JOURNEY'S END

A Novel

BILL JACK

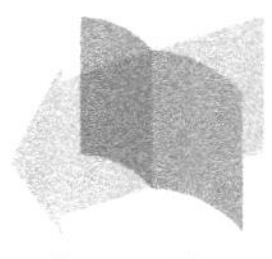

Chapbook Press

Chapbook Press
Schuler Books
2660 28th Street SE
Grand Rapids, MI 49512
(616) 942-7330
www.schulerbooks.com

Printed at Schuler Books in Grand Rapids, MI
on the Espresso Book Machine®

ISBN 13: 978-1-936243-16-7

ISBN 10: 1-936243-16-4

Cover art by Rebecca Sitterly

For Rebecca whose thoughtful insights, constant encouragement and true love gave me the courage to get to the end of the journey

For Kate whose energy and joy and humor has always been the centering force in my universe

I can't imagine the journey without the two of you.

ACKNOWLEDGMENTS

Any first time so-called author who finally sits down to write the first novel has the courage to do so because so many people have been there along the way to make sure the characters kept getting off the couch and back on to the page.

To Bob Dugoni, best selling author, teacher par excellence and incidental mentor who said: "Don't write to get published or to sell books or to become famous, write for your own self. That's the joy of it." That wisdom has been the foundation of Journey's End.

To sister Mary Sue whose love has endured and sustained all these many years.

To so many, many people who took the time to read the drafts, give advice almost all of which was taken, and offer encouragement whether they really meant it or not.

Especially to Debbie TenBrink whose patience and expertise has made the 2nd Edition a much better read.

Finally, to my friends. Your love in good times and bad and your willingness to see me for who I am and still be there for me has created immeasurable peace and joy.

WWJ   2012

THE JOURNEY

PROLOGUE

Beyond exhaustion, heartsick and weary to his very core. It had been the most important closing argument of his life.

And purely and simply, he had failed. Miserably and totally.

It was maybe a step or two, he would never know.

In those last split seconds, he heard what he thought were two words, maybe three. The first, clearly Davison. "Police!! Drop it!!" And then, maybe Alex, "Will!" Two pops, one like somebody kicked him in the kidney, the other to the back of his head, propelling it forward so his chin hit his chest. More pops.

Darkness, so deep as to be purple. So very deep.

He had lost.

CHAPTER ONE
ON THE EVE

Majorly into the joint venture, the two were jangled by the insistent ringing of the phone on the table next to them. Consideration was given to answering but only for an instant. This trip needed finishing and the plane landed. And so it was that the phone clicked to the answering machine and the joint venture was brought to a successful, albeit a tad interrupted, conclusion.

After a suitable respite to celebrate the end of the journey and to catch breaths, Will Bennett got up, put on a robe, and padded downstairs to replenish the Chardonnays. Alexandra Kennedy lay back on the pillows and reveled in the warmth of the aftermath.

Downstairs, Will checked the machine. No message, but the Caller ID identified the 703 Area Code. He thought for a minute about calling the number back, checked his watch, figured the time change, and opted for the wine and upstairs. The call back could wait until the day after next. It would be a long one.

Tomorrow was soon to come and it was time to have one more glass and to get some much needed sleep. His closing argument was in the morning.

CHAPTER TWO
TRIAL'S END

"All of us have hopes for our children, for their health and their future, for lives rich in texture and love…and all of us fear for their safety and their lives. It's what parents do." The older juror in the second row bowed his head.

"There is no one involved with this tragic case that doesn't feel the utmost compassion and caring for the Silkey family as they cope with the death of their daughter, their sister, their aunt. No one."

Will Bennett felt the familiar adrenaline rush as he warmed to the task ahead. They were listening to him and watching him and he knew, in his heart, that he had them.

"But that's not why we're here. We're here for you to decide if there was anything that could possibly have been done by the doctors caring for Ms. Silkey that would or could have made a difference and saved her life.

You each made a commitment to me, to Dr. Dell, and to this court that you would set your sympathies for her family aside and decide this matter on the evidence and the law Judge Crockett will give you in a moment. I hold you now to that commitment."

Bennett paused long enough to make eye contact with each one of the twelve members of the jury. Each, in turn, returned the look.

"Because you see, ladies and gentlemen, to believe the plaintiff's case is to believe the impossible." Another pause. "And here's why."

***

In the chambers of Judge Crockett, the Honorable Alexandra Kennedy listened to Bennett's closing argument over the speakers with a mixture of emotions, of respect because she knew how good he could be, of sadness because most of that talent had always been on the side of the defense where good lawyers could always be bought, but mostly because of the warmth of a deep and abiding love for the man. They had worked on the closing for much of the night prior to the sex and had fine-tuned it in the morning to practice the phrasing and the cadence and the tone. It had been Kennedy who'd suggested the "you must believe the impossible" language as the theme of the closing. It had sounded good that morning and sounded even better now.

What makes him so scary, she thought, is how sincere he is when he talks with that calmness that almost forbids the listener to do anything but agree with him. And what makes him even scarier is that he truly believes in the mission.

Wilson Bennett and Alexandra Kennedy had been married just over a year although they had, for lack of a better word, 'survived' a long distance relationship that had gone on…and off…and on…and off for the several years prior.

3

Bennett was from the Midwest, establishing a reputation there as one of the really good insurance defense trial lawyers in his state. Kennedy, born and raised in New Mexico, had first been a trial lawyer of significant reputation in her own right before being appointed by the Governor to the District Court five years ago.

They had met by chance at a trial lawyers' conference in San Diego seven years past. To hear Will tell it, it had been love at first sight when she had walked into the meeting room at the hotel. Truth be told, she didn't remember him that first time at all but had decided to keep that to herself. They had spent some time together in the same break out sessions and had gone their separate ways at the end of the conference with hardly a look back.

Within the year, there had been another serendipitous meeting, this time at an educational program for legal services attorneys at which they had both been invited to teach. Infrequent time together there and, after that, the beginning of an email correspondence that finally culminated in what they called the "neutral site"… Hartford.

And there, in three days and four nights, things had changed forever for them both. They ate one dinner out and spent the rest of the time ordering room service. From the moment Alexandra Kennedy stepped off the train from New York City where she'd been on a sabbatical, to the moment she got back on the train after a last long hug, it had been a time of pure magic. The passion started as the hotel room door opened. Marathon sessions of love making surprised them both at this stage of their lives and, in the moments they came up for air, they found an ability to talk at levels that seemed deeper and with a level of candor and frankness and sameness that could only be hoped for in a relationship that lasts a lifetime. It scared the bejesus out of both of them.

So it started. Five years of romance and passion, of anger and hurt feelings, of pulling the trigger on each other over and over, of frequent flier miles and weather delays, of continued passion and chemistry that kept each of them coming back around the corner almost despite themselves. Somebody once spoke about the difficulty of long distance relationships, but for them, it seemed to be the only way it could work.

Friends and family, in both camps, watched the ebb and flow of the couple as though they were watching a prize fight and were even more amazed when, after all the years, the two of them were still standing. Together.

Exhausted by the times apart and passion lost through distance, they married in Santa Fe in a quiet ceremony in the United States District Court chambers of Kennedy's friend, Judge Roberta Chavez. Contrary to the thought that marriage takes away the insecurity that makes relationships work, Will and Alex found they had had so much insecurity over the last five years that finally being married gave them a peace they'd never experienced before.

The timing had worked. Bennett's daughter, Grace, was a senior in college and thinking about law school. Kennedy had been appointed to the bench and no longer endured the stresses of a trial practice for the first time in her 23 year career. She tried more cases than ever before but, as the judge, she got to sleep very well the night before. Bennett took the New Mexico bar exam and, miracle of miracles at his age, passed. Not by much, mind you, but close enough to get sworn in.

One of the good defense firms in Albuquerque needed some gray hair to try cases and welcomed Bennett as a full partner. Will knew it didn't hurt to be married to a district court judge but soon found that juries would listen to him as well in Albuquerque as in the Midwest. He moved into Kennedy's townhouse in Old Town and they began what they both hoped would be years of happiness and joy. There would be bad times, of course, but they also knew that the chemistry that had held them together for so long and through so much, ought to hold now that they were finally together. Realistic certainly, pragmatic, of course, they wanted to make this one work.

*****

Kennedy's reverie was broken when she heard her husband gear up for the "sit down" moment.

"And finally this, ladies and gentlemen, even knowing your sympathies for the family, even knowing your sadness over the death of Jennifer Silkey, and even knowing you can never undo that sadness, you must find for Robert Dell. The law requires it, the truth requires it…and justice requires it Bob Dell and I will be waiting for your verdict."

In the courtroom, Bennett paused and again looked each juror in the eye. In the silence of the next several seconds, each again met his gaze. He gathered his papers from the lectern and walked back to counsel table. Plaintiff's counsel quickly stood to break the silence and start her rebuttal.

***

Kennedy thought her husband to still be a handsome man, although she was never quite sure of her objectivity. Average height, still reasonably trim at age 56 and, with beautiful silver hair, she thought he looked like a trial lawyer should. His face had an openness about it that could never quite hide whatever he was thinking, and beautiful brown eyes, and a smile that still melted her heart. Most of the time. Bright but not overly, confident but hardly arrogant, and always always well prepared, he had done well not only for himself and his clients but for the young lawyers he mentored both in his prior life and now here in Albuquerque. And now, one more time, he had done what he could to bring closure for his client.

She got up and returned to her chambers without listening to the rebuttal. It would go on for some time. Judge Crockett would instruct the jury and then the hard part would come - waiting for the verdict.

Shortly before noon, Judge Kennedy's Case Manager, Karen Stillson knocked on her door. Karen had followed Alex to the bench from private practice and, in addition to being the best anybody could be at managing the chaos of the Judge's busy docket, she was also Alex's best woman friend. "There's some thing here to see you that looks like it needs a hug," Karen said.

"Send it on in, Karen."

A moment later, Bennett walked in and she felt that familiar warmth she always felt when he first walked into a room. She walked around her desk and they held each other just like that first embrace at the train station in Hartford. She felt a slight press in the front of his pants, knew first hand that trying cases was the most powerful aphrodisiac in the world despite the bone numbing fatigue that comes at the end of a long trial. She smiled with the sure knowledge that the night wouldn't pass without some action, someplace in the townhouse, win or lose.

From Bennett's point of view, she was the anchor that finally had given meaning to his life after all the stops and starts, all the insecurities, all the relationships that had ended badly. He leaned back so he could see the face that had captured him all those years.

She was one of those women lucky enough to get better looking as they got older. She had high cheekbones, smooth skin albeit with some lines around the clear blue eyes, and the legs of a dancer that women half her age would kill for. Though she held a few more pounds than in her hey day and she was letting a little more of the gray show in her blonde hair, she was still able to turn heads of kids young enough to be her sons. Born scrabble poor and having worked her way through college and law school, at 53 she made no apologies for the journey of life and figured each line and each pound had been damn well earned.

The old adage of "...never elect or appoint a judge unless they have to take a cut in pay" was never so appropriate than in Judge Kennedy's case. The fire and passion that had characterized her as a trial lawyer made way for a calm, measured judicial demeanor that surprised even her closest friends. She kept many of her trademarks from private practice. Cowboy boots under the black robe, the Annie Oakley poster behind her desk, her uncle's lariat in the glass

9

case on the wall. You could never take the cowgirl out of the essence of whom she would always be.

And now with marriage, the wild side of Alex Kennedy had also settled down. Still fire and passion in the bedroom but now more than content to share it only with her husband.

Holding hands, Will and Alex talked about the trial. But for the verdict, it was over, and they could have their life back. It was the absolute absorption into every aspect of her life that had finally tipped Kennedy into accepting the judgeship and which now, more than ever, made it difficult for Bennett to gear up again and again.

"Maybe this'll be the last one," Will said quietly.

"Maybe so." But she knew better. He would go on. It was all he knew. He would talk about alimony and college and graduate school tuition and his retirement accounts being trashed, but the real reason was that he was good at it, he was respected for it, it gave him the freedom to teach at the law school, and hopefully it gave him the precious time with Alex and their new life together.

They kissed. Then Will left to join his client, Dell's wife, and the insurance adjuster for lunch.

4:30 that afternoon while Judge Kennedy was on the bench listening to the last of what seemed like a never ending litany of arraignments, Karen Stillson came in through the judicial entrance and slipped the judge a note. Her heart skipped a beat. The note read simply:

"The jury's back."

CHAPTER THREE
THE DEFENSE RESTS

They lay side by side in the big bed, legs splayed, holding hands and catching their breaths.

Finally able to breathe normally after a few minutes, Alex whispered,

"Congrats again."

"It's over, that's the part to be happy about. It's just over."

Actually, it was a little better than that. The jury had gone out just before noon and apparently decided Bernalillo County could afford one more lunch for the hard working citizenry of the jury. They went to lunch, came back, deliberated for a little less than three hours and rang the bell announcing they had a verdict.

Seated at counsel table with his client, Will Bennett felt that familiar tension and apprehension. It had lessened over time as winning or losing had become less important than simply doing the best he could. Winning was always better than losing, for sure, but as long as he could look himself in the mirror and say 'you did the best you could' losing was less the devil than it had been.

"All rise. Court is back in session, the Honorable Daniel Crockett presiding." Judge Crockett entered from his chambers. "Please remain standing until the jury is seated."

Moments later, the jury entered from the side door connecting to the jury room and filed in one by one to take their now familiar chairs. Bennett studied them carefully. Jurors often looked at the side they had voted for. Not this group. Impassive, they stared straight ahead until told they could sit.

Judge Crockett asked, "Ladies and gentlemen of the jury. Have you reached a verdict and, if so, would the foreperson please rise?"

Juror number 3, the humanities professor from the University of New Mexico rose and in a strong voice said, "We have, Your Honor."

Tension. Bennett put his hand on his client's arm. Not a sound in the courtroom.

"Very well, Madam Foreperson. The verdict form, please?"

"Yes, Your Honor." She opened the piece of paper. "Question No. 1: Was Robert Dell, MD professionally negligent in the treatment of Jennifer Silkey?" The foreperson paused as though she understood the drama of the moment. "Answer: Yes." She paused and looked directly at Dr. Dell. "Question No. 2: Was the defendant's professional negligence a proximate cause of the death of Jennifer Silkey?" She paused again, now clearly enjoying her moment in the sun. "No."

There was an almost audible whoosh of released air.

"Do you wish to have the jury polled, Ms. Delacorte?"

"Yes, Your Honor." In a hushed voice almost too quiet to be heard.

In turn, Judge Crockett asked each of the jurors whether they agreed with the verdict. Each responded affirmatively. At the end, Judge Crockett thanked the jury for their service and excused them. In the quiet of the courtroom, Judge Crockett asked counsel whether there was anything else that needed to be on the record. Both Bennett and Delacorte said no.

The judge spent a few moments extolling the virtues of the jury system primarily for the benefit of the clients, praised the efforts of the lawyers, and announced that Court was adjourned. All in the courtroom rose as he left the bench. Will Bennett, who the whole time had had his best courtroom face on, went over to Irene Delacorte, shook her hand, shook Jennifer Silkey's father's hand, and then returned to counsel table. Will whispered to his client, "Let's get out of here, Bob. I'll clean up what's left later." He took him by the arm, went through the gates of the well back to the spectator rows, gathered up Dell's wife and the adjuster, took the stairs, left the building and went to the place across the street where they had lunched. Only when they were seated in one of the back booths did Bennett say to his client, "Congratulations, Bob, you deserve this, you truly do." Both Dell and his wife had tears in their eyes. "But why negligence?" The two of them in unison.

Bennett paused for just a moment to say just the right thing. In his mind, he turned over the various answers that might work. Finally, "Because they knew you didn't do anything wrong but felt it was something they could leave with the family. Only thing that makes sense."

Dr. Dell and his wife looked satisfied although Bennett could tell the adjuster wasn't buying it for a heartbeat. She knew they had dodged a very large bullet. Dell had missed a pulmonary embolus that was pretty much clear as day. But there was little that could have been done to save the young woman's life. Hence, justice.

More pleasantries, tearful good byes from the Dells, promises to have Bennett and the adjuster and their spouses "out to the club for dinner one of these days." Promises all of them knew were bullshit even as they were said.

Wilson Bennett walked back to the courthouse to pick up his file and briefcase. Out to the club my ass. 'lo Bob and Martha, love to have you meet my malpractice lawyer – really pulled my ass out of the ringer, right-o, Will?' Right-o, Bob. Clearly time to go home. Cynicism in full bloom, it was time for a martini.

He walked through the door of the townhouse. Said hey to The High Jinks, a tiny little 7 lb. stray cat that had

15

wandered into Alex's life six years ago and never left, and saw the note on the frig: 'It's in the freezer.' Sure enough, a very large martini 'up' stood on the top shelf. Bennett grabbed it, took a very long, very lovely sip, and walked up the stairs to the bedroom, dropping articles of clothing along the way. The bedroom was dark in the early October evening save for the candles lit around the room, Bill Evans on the CD, and Alexandra Kennedy in her favorite teddy lying on the bed, legs ever so slightly apart, with that smile of hers that could stop him across a crowded room.

"Come to the cowgirl, Will".

It was the one pure thing that had never wavered in all of the years together, in all of the ups and downs, or as Alex liked to put it, the "ins and outs". There had, from the very beginning, been plenty of the "ins and outs" and they often laughed at how often they still wanted and needed them.

A last sip of the gin and Will joined his wife.

***

Some time later the phone rang. Both of them knew with absolute certainty who it was. As Will leaned over to pick it up, Alex whispered, "At least this time he had the good sense to wait for the sex to be over."

What neither of them could know was that this phone call would forever change their lives.

CHAPTER FOUR
THE CALL FOR HELP

"Sam? How are you, man?" Bennett asked.

"Will, I gotta talk to you. It's worse, much much worse." The familiar voice from 2,000 miles away.

Bennett pulled himself up in the bed noting that, in Virginia, it was 9:30. It was not particularly late for a call like this but it meant two things. One, his truly very best friend in the world until Alex was not home and, two, he'd been drinking. The first because Sam would never call him from home with his wife in earshot, especially in these last weeks. And two, because in these same last weeks, the late night calls had been punctuated with slurred words and incoherent sentences. Will knew his best friend was in some sort of very bad deal but Sam had been anything but forthcoming. Maybe tonight.

As Alex got up and put a robe on, Will gestured at his now empty glass with a pleading look.

"Sure, man, this is a good time." Hoping against hope that Alex would understand that a second martini was now critical. "Sam, talk to me." Propping the pillows up against the headboard.

"It's awful, Will, headaches every day, and nothing touches them. I keep thinking tumor."

Will Bennett could hear the fear in his friend's voice and it scared him.

He had met Sam Greenberg at the end of their second year at George Washington Law School in D.C. A group of six or seven irreverent students would meet in the J. Edgar Hoover Conference Room in the library supposedly to study for exams, kibitz, play matchbook football, and pretty much do anything but study. Activities during the all too frequent breaks would include the football, turning off all the lights and throwing a neon Frisbee around the room, or, in particularly tense times, tossing an orange around the walls at the top of the room until it broke. And while it was the breakee who had to catch the mess, it was the breaker who had to buy a round of coffee for the assembled group at the next break. Sam Greenberg had wandered into that like minded group of mis and mal contents one day. Bennett had seen him around, had had a couple of classes with him, and had seen him in the Union with a large circle of friends but had never actually talked to him.

His presence at first cast a pall upon the group that had been together since the second semester of first year and the games quickly came to a halt. But as the exam period wore on and Sam showed up day after day, the games rekindled and Sam became a regular. Terrible at matchbook football, worse at the orange toss, his saving grace was his humor and his warmth. And by the end of second year exams, Sam Greenberg, this tall swarthy Jewish guy from New York City and Wilson Bennett, about as cornbread a white guy from the Midwest as you could get, had started a friendship that would last a lifetime.

Third year they were inseparable, beers and hard boiled eggs at the tavern where the not-quite-so-serious law students would gather, tennis whenever they had some time and sometimes when they didn't, ski trips to Pennsylvania (the "pimple mountains") when, on the way back, they would swear they'd never end up like those "losers" in suits and ties commuting to and from dead end jobs. It was a connection that neither understood very well but that they treasured because, for both of them, it was special and it was real.

At some point they had tried to analyze their friendship and why it had prospered. The differences were many and profound. Samuel Greenberg from a Jewish background in New York City, parents divorced when he was little, much time spent in boarding schools through high school, educated in the East, and choosing to stay in the DC area after graduation. Obsessive compulsive to the absolute max, making certain that each piece of his life was in perfect order from a pristine home life to color coding items of clothing (socks, shirts, even underwear) to an office that looked like a paperless photo-op for a business magazine.

19

Wilson Bennett was born and raised in a Midwest homogenous city, parents professional and together, growing up in the safety of home and a suburban high school, educated in Michigan, and going back to the Midwest pretty much as soon as he could after law school, tired of the frenetic pace of the east coast. In contrast to Sam's OCD, Will liked to think of himself as "free form" in terms of neatness; going to work in the morning with one black sock and one blue one was considered a fashion victory.

But they had seen something in each other that resonated – as long as they didn't try to ruin it by ever being roommates.

In the years to come, they had stayed the closest of friends, thousands of miles apart but still just a phone call away. They had survived marriages, divorces, cancers of loved ones, deaths of parents, fights between the two of them that often lasted weeks until one of them could stand it no longer, and an openness and honesty that sustained them both through the years.

It was a friendship that had endured. And one that Wilson Bennett would do anything to keep. Even if it meant post-coital-interruptus.   Or, like last night, intra-coital-interruptus.

He already knew the answer but Will asked whether Sam had seen the neurologist. "Three times this week, she tells me the MRI is normal, the CT is normal but something is so wrong," Sam said. "I don't know how much more of this I can take."

"Sam, listen to me. There is nothing wrong physically. It is something else." Bennett went through the usual list: stress at work, marriage, concern over his daughter Rachel, was there anything that could be doing this to him? His best friend said no, no, no and no. And the conversation ended in frustration just like all the others. They hung up with expressions of love and support but no solution. Alex walked back in on cue carrying a tray with a martini, a glass of Pinot Grigio, and a pile of shrimp, some sourdough bread, and cocktail sauce.

"Same old, same old?"

"Same old. Come to bed, babe. Classic movie?"

The phone rang. Hoping against hope that it was anybody but Sam, Will picked it up. Sam again, his voice so quiet and strained, it was difficult to hear him.

"Will, any chance of you and me meeting at the lake house? I need to see you, need to be away, I'm losing it." Bennett thought about it and turned to Alex who busied herself fiddling with the tray and the remote. It could probably work. He had scheduled the trial to last for another week not because it would but because, over the years, there was decompression time that he built in after a trial much like a deep sea diver coming up for air. Different "bends" but the bends nevertheless. And the lake house had been empty for several weeks. It was a remnant of his life in Michigan, a modest home bought years ago with a spectacular view of Lake Michigan and a place where he and then Alex (and often times Sam with or without family) found great peace.

Will put his hand over the phone and looked at Alex. "Lake house for a few days with Sam?" he whispered. "I think you better," she said. "This isn't getting any better."

"All right, Sam. Give me 24 hours to get things straight and let's figure on getting there mid afternoon on Wednesday." Sam's voice improved, "I love you man. I'll email my reservation times. I love you, Will." And the phone went dead without even a goodbye.

She looked at her lover straight on. "Will boy, there is something seriously wrong with your friend. He's gay. He's having an affair. Sharon is having an affair. He's losing his job. He's being chased by gangsters. He's become a Republican and can't handle it. Something."

It would take weeks before they knew how close she had come.

CHAPTER FIVE
THE LAKE HOUSE

Wilson Bennett hoped his game face kept his shock from his friend as Sam Greenberg walked down the ramp to meet him at the airport. Stooped and slow, Bennett thought he had aged twenty five years in the four months since they'd seen each other. Very dark glasses hid his eyes but Sam's skin was sallow to the point of almost a hepatitis yellow, his tall frame now gaunt with weight loss and, for a moment, Will reconsidered all those times he'd assured his friend that he was healthy. This was not healthy. They hugged and Bennett felt like he had his arms around the Scarecrow, careful not to squeeze too hard for fear of breaking something.

Sam took his glasses off for a moment only to shock Will a second time. Eyes red with fatigue, sunken into his face almost as though somebody had pushed them farther into his sockets. Deciding "You look like shit" was a little too harsh at least for now, he kept the conversation to a superficial minimum trying to get his emotions under control. Jesus, I hope he's not thinking the same thing about me. They talked of the plane flights and weather and Alex and Grace and Sam's wife, Sharon, and the Greenberg's daughter, Rachel, gathered Sam's bags and got to the rental car.

In the hour and a half from the airport to the lake house, there was a weirdly out of character lack of conversation, a quick stop at the grocery store in town for provisions, and then on to the lake. Rounding the last bend on a beautiful October afternoon that the Michigan Chamber always marketed but seldom delivered, Bennett's pulse slowed perceptibly as it always did when he got a first look at the incredible blue green of Lake Michigan. It was calm and sunny and warm. And not even that could lift his friend's spirits.

"Headache?" Bennett asked afraid that his friend had dozed off behind the glasses.

"Bad," came the answer. They got to the place, got it unlocked, got the pump and water heater running and Will ordered his friend to lie down for a nap. It was in part for Sam but mostly so he could get his own self back. As quietly as possible, he checked the place out, filled the bird feeders, made sure everything worked, then settled out on the deck to bask in the warmth of the fall sun and wondered what to do about the man who, after his daughter and Alex, meant more to him than anyone. He tried to call home for moral support, got the message machine, and decided his wife was ducking him. He knew better but somehow liked the feel of it.

As the sun grew low in the West with the promise of one of the great Michigan sunsets ahead and with the fall chill creeping in on the end of the day, Sam appeared, with better color and brighter eyes, and a smile for the first time since he'd gotten off the plane. He took a very deep breath.

"Will, I love it here, it's always been the place when all else is in shambles that I know I can come and get well." It was an often expressed comment but this time clearly far more important and far more deeply felt. Bennett felt the same way about the place and even though life had taken him 1800 miles away, it was always like coming home.

He fixed the two of them drinks, a martini on the rocks for him and some white wine for Sam, some heavy hors d'ouvres as an excuse for dinner, and they settled in to watch the sunset, listen to some jazz and talk. Sam spoke mostly about the last weeks and months, of the onslaught of headaches that had started as an annoyance and now had come to the point of almost crippling him, of the stress it had put on Sharon and their marriage, of the time away from his work going to doctors and simply being unable to cope, of not having a clue as to why. Bennett thought his friend remarkably self absorbed as he refilled their drinks, and then caught himself. Shit, if I looked as bad as he does, I'd be a tad self absorbed myself.

With Alex's intuition that there was something going on way beyond the headaches of every day life sitting on his right shoulder, Will broached the topic.

"Sam, I need to be as straight with you as I can. So shut up and listen. There is nothing wrong with you physically so what this is is something deeper and darker than either you know about or are willing to share." Greenberg shook his head in denial.

"I don't know what it is and I can't help unless I know but let's start at the top. Sharon? You guys OK?"

A pause and a deep breath. "No, we're not OK, Will. At first, I thought it was 'cause she was so stressed out about me and what's going on." His head dropped and then his voice, "Now I think maybe she's seeing someone." A very long pause as each took a drink. One of the great lessons of a trial lawyer is knowing when to shut up and listen. Bennett let the silence be.

"I don't know for sure. Ask her about it and she denies it. But I don't know. Lost some weight, big exercise program, new haircut and clothes," his voice tailed off again. "I've been pretty awful, Will, these last months. I'm gone a lot on business and with the headaches, not worth a shit at home at anything. Not sure I'd even blame her." Let the silence be, Will. "A week ago, she talked about a 'trial separation' to give us time 'to work it out'. Now that Rachel's in college, there just isn't much left for us."

As gently as he could, Bennett asked, "Is that what's eating you?"

"I don't think so. It's where we are but not just 'cause of the headaches. I really think she still loves me even if she is fucking around. I just think she's tired of me. Tired of me being like this."

There's really not a lot of places you go with that, Bennett thought to himself. But Sam at least was talking. Conversation trailed off and, within minutes, Bennett had talked his friend into getting to bed. It was only 9:00 P.M. but the sun was gone and the evening cooling down.

Will poured himself a nightcap of Jameson's neat, got a coat, and went out on the deck to watch the stars come out and to call Alex.

CHAPTER SIX
RESPITE

For the next three days, Will and Sam enjoyed the lingering Indian Summer of warm and sunny days, cool nights, and the kind of quiet togetherness that comes only from friendships that have lasted so long that neither has expectations of the other. They walked on the beach and through the woods, rode bikes in the rolling farmlands of western Michigan, hit some tennis balls and even played a round of golf.

Throughout, they talked about all of the facets of Sam's life: his marriage, his work, his health and Will gently tried to coax out of his friend all that was going on in his busy life. He had known Sharon Greenberg for as long as she and Sam had been together; he could see her frustrated and even angry at Sam's worries about his headaches and his OCD, but he really couldn't see her as the type to run from the issues of her marriage. If anything, she would be far more apt to confront him head on and work together. It sounded as though she had tried to do that although life-long compulsiveness to the max and headaches without reason were not the easiest of issues to cope with.

As for work, Sam thought that things were percolating along pretty well save for the time spent recently going to doctors. A long time president of a trade association promoting environmentally clean products, he had traveled extensively, was often invited to the Hill to testify, and all in all, seemed satisfied with where he was. Earlier on, he had bemoaned the journey his life had taken and wondered where the idealism of their years together as law clerks with the legal services program had gone. But then every child of the '60s and '70s thought that from time to time, Will had told him, and as the years had gone by, he had seemed more content. So to Will, it didn't feel like work was a major player in the malaise.

And as for his health, nothing in western medicine had been able to explain what clearly were crippling headaches. Every single objective test known to man had been negative and Sam had turned to the shrinks. And their conclusion? For a New York City Jewish guy from a dysfunctional family, he seemed pretty normal. Sure he had the normal stresses of life everybody has; not enough sex in the marriage; a woman who doesn't completely understand what he does but keeps the home fires burning; an over-achieving, perfectionist daughter who he loved almost too much; significant debt trying to keep ends met living in Northern Virginia; a private school for Rachel; a job that too often kept him from home; etc. etc. The usual stuff.

Will would later tell Alex that it was one of the best times he had ever enjoyed with Sam. As each day passed, he

29

saw in his friend the lifting of the shroud of depression. The headaches seemed better, he overheard him laughing on a call to Sharon about something in their life, he walked straighter, and even his skin looked healthier. On the last Saturday night, they went to the local tavern known for its friendship and ambience and talked about the future days for Sam. And whether it was the drinks or the tavern or the three days together, Will went to bed that night convinced that Sam Greenberg had turned a corner and that, certainly with the help of some major anti-depressants and pain meds, he was on the road back.

Sunday morning they drove to the airport. Sam seemed calm and a little quiet but, all told, still on a good roll. Only at security when they said goodbye did Will once again see a look in his friend's eyes that nonplussed him. He couldn't tell exactly what it was. Worry? Fear? Pain? No way to tell but after their last hug and after he watched Sam walk down the hall to security, Wilson Bennett was left with the very unsettled feeling that the lake house was a respite not a cure.

Bennett spent the rest of Sunday at a service at his old church, brunch with some friends and ex-partners catching up on their lives and then caught the last flight out to Albuquerque, uneventful and routine from all the backs and forths of the old days. But he couldn't shake the feeling that, as much as they had talked and as well as he knew Sam, there was still something that hadn't gotten said, hadn't gotten exposed to the light, and still was out there to be dealt with.

Alex was asleep when he got home and he tucked himself in with the warmth of his lover's body next to him, skin on skin, drifting off to a deep sleep without dreams. To a next morning of love making that reflected too much time away from each other, an occasion that they tolerated less and less.

The next couple of days settled into the rhythm of busy lives and jobs. The lake house became a warm and hazy memory. There was only one short voicemail from Sam saying he'd gotten home and would do his best.

That was it - until Wednesday when Rachel Greenberg called him in hysterics to tell him her mother was dead, murdered, and that her father had disappeared without a trace.

CHAPTER SEVEN
COMING TOGETHER

Wilson Bennett carefully put the phone back in the cradle after trying to comfort Rachel about something for which there could be no comfort and trying to get his own mind around the unimaginable. He ended the call by telling Rachel that he and Alex would get East as quickly as they could.

He called Alex but she was on the bench early and he asked Karen to have her call as soon as she possibly could. She asked about interrupting and Will said absolutely not. He needed to get his own head set about what had happened before anything else. For the next several minutes, he sat in his chair, Do Not Disturb on the phone, and, layer by layer, took in and processed what he had just heard.

Sharon Greenberg shot and killed in her own home, discovered in the early morning when a neighbor became alarmed at the Greenbergs' dog barking in the house and called the police. His best friend of thirty plus years gone missing, no sign of him at home or work, both cars still in the driveway. Rachel Greenberg called by the Alexandria police with news so horrific that Bennett thought idly there must be a special kind of straw draw to pull that duty. Rachel's anguished call to her father's best friend on her way home with a friend from college. None of it made sense but there it was, news so huge it sucked the air out of his office.

Karen Stillson knew Bennett well and Alexandra Kennedy better and the tone of Bennett's voice left her only one choice. She wrote a note to the Judge, went through the judicial door behind the bench and slipped her the note that said simply: "Take a break, Will needs you." In the middle of arraignments on what was euphemistically called Zoo Day by the lawyers and judges, Judge Kennedy abruptly announced the morning break 45 minutes early and quickly left the bench leaving lawyers, prisoners, and family members struggling to their feet in her rush to get to chambers.

She called his direct number, got the DND, called the general number and got his assistant who was still blissfully unaware that her life, like theirs, was about to irrevocably change. Liz knocked on the door, entered without waiting for a response and found Will Bennett frozen in his chair. "The Judge is on the phone, Will," she paused, "Will?" He looked at her and she would later swear he looked right through her. He picked up the phone and she closed the door quietly.

Judge Kennedy hung up and sat quietly in her chambers. She and her husband had both been blessed with the same trait that trial lawyers found indispensable – the worse the news, the calmer they got. And she was calm. Will had told her what he knew in a voice too very quiet, filled with

33

pain and loss. Will told her he would try to get them out still that day and she would try to get coverage for Zoo Day.

"We'll get through this, Will." Kennedy's voice just as quiet as she hung up.

Judge Kennedy took a deep breath, steadied herself, and returned to the bench. Neither lawyers nor defendants saw any difference in her. Only Karen Stillson knew things were suddenly upside down. Alex had told her she'd need coverage starting in the afternoon and continuing for God knew how long.

Three blocks away, Will told Liz what had happened. If you're going to work for a trial lawyer, the same trait of calmness in the face of the storm is all a part of the job, and in a heartbeat, Liz was back to the professional she'd always been. Liz and Will pored over the calendar for the next days figuring out what could be adjourned or cancelled and what would need coverage. Associates were rounded up and put on notice that they were to be at Liz's beck and call in what hopefully would only be days and not weeks to come. Liz checked on flights, couldn't get them out that day and booked them early the next morning.

Shortly before noon, Will packed some papers and his laptop, hugged Liz good-bye and, back bent, walked to the parking garage.

What he couldn't get his head around was where his best friend was. For the tenth time, he called Sam's cell phone and got voice mail. Will had kidded Sam about how depressed he sounded on the message and Sam had promised to get it fixed. But it was still the same old Eeyore voice of doom. Will had left the one message and this time was told the mailbox was full. Others had the same number and were trying the same thing.

At the town house, Will let himself in, closed doors windows and drapes, made a pot of tea and tried to make a plan in the cool darkness of the living room. He called Sam's office again and got the same message from Tracy as before. She hadn't seen or heard from him. But this time there was an ominous footnote. The Alexandria homicide detectives had been to see her. Will hung up and felt like he'd swallowed a baseball. Of course they would be looking for him if only to tell him that somebody had murdered his wife. But a murdered woman in her home and no sign of her husband would also make him a very special "person of interest." He called Rachel's cell phone, got her voice mail, told her when they'd be in the next afternoon and to call him.

A key in the lock and Alex Kennedy walked in. She had stopped at the co-op and gotten food for supper. A bottle of Pinot Grigio under her arm. She unpacked and came in and sat down next to her husband. There had been a time in their

35

relationship that news like this would have been handled individually and not by the partnership but those days were long gone. She was in it and would be to the end. There had been a time when he would have said something stupid like "you don't have to go, you know" but those days as well were also a thing of the past. She was in it and would be to the end. Period. And he loved her all the more for it.

Alex and Will spent the next couple of hours noodling over what they knew and didn't know, what scenarios were likely and what weren't, what outcomes were likely and what weren't. Alex was a degree separated from it because it was his friend long before her who was in trouble and that gave her an objectivity that was invaluable.

It went like this. "Do you think Sam killed her?" From Will's perspective, it was unfathomable but it clearly had occurred to the homicide detectives in Virginia. And so it was on the table. They talked a lot about the conversations at the lake house that Will had shared and whether Sam had confirmed the affair when he'd gotten home and had killed his wife in a rage.

Sharon had been killed and Sam kidnapped, that was another scenario.

Will liked that one a lot better except for the assumption that he had been kidnapped and, as far as they knew, had not been heard from. Plus he could be dead by now.

Sam was on an unexpected business trip out of town and had forgotten to tell his office. Sharon had been surprised and killed by a burglar. That worked for Will as well except that it made no sense. Sam Greenberg's OCD would never let him forget to tell Tracy where he was. Okay. Sam had an early morning meeting, had left the house, and Sharon was killed after that by a stranger. That worked except Rachel had said both cars were in the driveway.

Will's cell phone rang and he rushed to pick it up. It was Rachel. Her voice was high pitched and trembly and Will could hear the tears in her voice. She had gotten to Virginia, stopped at a friend's house nearby, and then driven to her home. It was taped off as a crime scene and a uniformed officer stood watch. A Crime Investigation Unit van was parked in the driveway. She had met with the Alexandria homicide detectives who came to the house after being called by the patrolman, had been taken to the hospital morgue where she had identified her mother, and then had been interviewed by the police.

Rachel now knew the following. The police dispatch had gotten the 911 call at 6:48 a.m. and a patrol car had arrived at 7:02. There was no answer at either the front or back doors, no evidence of forcible entry and so the police broke a window in the back door and went in. There was nothing unusual until they got to the master bedroom where they had found Sharon Greenberg dressed in a T shirt and panties on the bed with what was apparently a gunshot wound to the chest. They checked for life, found none, secured the scene and called the Crime Investigation Unit, the Medical Examiner and the homicide team. There was no trace of the weapon and, other than the dog, nobody else in the house. Interviewed neighbors had heard nothing like a gunshot or any disturbance and nobody could remember the last time they had actually seen Sam. Attempts to reach him via his office and cell phone had been unsuccessful. The detectives had talked to his secretary who had expected him in and had no idea where he was. Alexandria Homicide had ruled out accident or suicide. It was murder and they very much wanted to talk to Rachel's father. So did Rachel.

So did Will.

CHAPTER EIGHT
HEADING EAST

As late as the reservations were made, Alex and Will were relegated to the second to last row, middle and window. Usually the king of chivalry to take the middle, Will took one look at the aisle passenger and edged into the window seat to be alone with his thoughts. Alex next wedged in past the older woman who smiled apologetically as she asked for the belt extender from the flight attendant to fit around a truly massive girth. The two of them settled in for what promised to be a very long two and a half hours. Discouraging conversation with even each other, they both donned the privacy of headphones and iPods.

Normally prepared with newspapers or work or a crossword puzzle book or a novel, Will Bennett instead spent most of the time simply staring out the window with John Coltrane's sad saxophone ballads as company. This time, instead of playing out various scenarios of doom, his mind allowed itself to wander through his life with Sam, remembering the first tentative steps of friendship and all that had gone on between the two of them over the years. Years ago, after way too many drinks, the two of them had promised each other they would always be there for one another no matter what.

And it truly had been that way. It had been Will in these last months who had been Sam's bedrock as he sorted through his physical and mental struggles. But in years gone by, the roles had been reversed and Sam had been there on many a long call or many a long walk when Will had poured his heart and soul out over the injustice or the sadness or the anger that had gotten in the way of his journey. Never judgmental, never angry, always the friend. And now it was his turn - only this was much, much worse. Will remembered out of nowhere the line from a song now long banished to oldies stations: "And you can call on me until the day you die."

They landed in Minneapolis and Alex helped her fellow passenger out of her seat.

An hour layover in the Twin Cities with dual Starbucks to fortify them and on to National. This time, a skinnier seat mate and Will's chivalry had returned him to the center seat and they spoke of a plan when they got there. Liz had made reservations with Hertz and a place to stay at the Alexandria Holiday Inn in the Old Town historic district for the foreseeable future. Kennedy's inn of choice was the Holiday Inn Express for reasons never understood but always abided by but there was no such animal any where close to where they needed to be. They had broken one of their cardinal rules of never checking luggage but were finally rewarded when, only 45 minutes after landing, their bags appeared.

5 P.M. Virginia time, they had their car and were checked into the hotel.

It was time to call Rachel.

CHAPTER NINE
DINNER

Will and Rachel met at Friday's for dinner. Alex and Will had talked over how to handle seeing her for the first time and both independently came to the conclusion that he was better going alone. She had nominally been his god child although that had never been what it should have been. Too many miles, too busy to take the time. Nevertheless, he had watched her grow from a temperamental spoiled young child "with issues" to an accomplished young woman with potential that only waited to be fulfilled. A youth orchestra violinist, varsityvolley ball player, National Merit Winner, partial scholarship to UVA, until only hours ago she had been riding a crest of success and happiness. That had now changed forever, her mom dead and her dad missing. At least for now an orphan.

He watched her as she approached the table.

Rachel Greenberg looked better than he'd expected but there were still dark circles under her brown eyes and a nervousness about her that he had not seen in years. Hardly unexpected, Will thought, because nothing was, nor ever would be, normal again.

"So…" Bennett asked after a long tearful hug and a chance to order iced tea for the two of them. Rachel had spent the day with her friends and families and had had no further contact with the police. She had been to the funeral home and had helped make arrangements for the funeral at the Temple on Saturday. She seemed to Will remarkably grown up and mature as she spoke of the plans, the music, who would speak, how the luncheon in the Temple basement would look, what her mom's obituary would say. She was talking about the minutia only to forestall tears that were so very close to the surface, a façade a heartbeat away from dissolving in tears.

Rachel had set up a meeting at the house the next morning with the Alexandria homicide detectives, herself, and her god father and his wife, the judge. Sharon's body was gone, of course, moved to the morgue for the autopsy, and the crime scene investigation teams had been all over the house. So it was safe for Rachel to go in but not alone, not after what had happened.

Will and Rachel spoke of the mundane, the funeral, the sale of the house, what to do with Lucky, the Lab who had first alerted the neighbors to the nightmare inside, when Rachel would get back to school. She was an only child with both sets of grandparents gone and only an uncle on Sam's side who had, according to her dad, been MIA for over a decade. Sharon also an only child. Rachel had yet to understand how lonely life would look as the days and weeks passed.

Dishes cleared and the 800 pound gorilla still to talk about.

"Will, where's my dad?" Tears flowing freely now.

"I have no clue, Rachel. I saw him last weekend at the lake house and he seemed OK. Worried about his headaches, worried about everything. Putting my place in order like always," a mutual acknowledgment of her father's well known OCD, "but I thought pretty good for an old guy."

"Did he talk about mom at all and how they were doing and what was going on with them now that I was gone and were they still happy and were they doing things together and...and..." She stopped, dropped her head, and Rachel Greenberg was no longer a mature adult faced with an unimaginable tragedy but a child faced with a horror not only unimaginable but without anchor or center or logic or reason. Quiet tears continued that were nearly as wrenching to Will as to her.

It gave Bennett just enough time to get himself pulled together wondering why the hell Alex wasn't with him and then starting in. On a lie.

"Like always, we talked about everything, Rachel. You know us well enough to know that. Jobs, the past, the future, you, Grace, life, Republicans. And we talked about your mom and how hard these last weeks had been on her, first with you moving out, and then your dad's medical stuff.

But I thought it was all sort of normal stuff for the two of them."

It did not take a rocket surgeon to figure out what was going through her head, the heads of the homicide detectives, and his own and Alex's. Sharon Greenberg had been shot to death in her own house, in her own bedroom, her husband gone missing, and a ridiculously high percentage of murders done by somebody who knows the victim. And the overwhelming majority of those a part of the ever spiraling cycle of domestic violence. Hello?

And so The Lie. As Will sat with Rachel Greenberg, he felt shame and sadness and anger at himself because the one thing he had promised Alexandra Kennedy was that he'd finally be honest about anything and everything. And he had done his very best and liked where it had taken him. Now here he was, in the crisis of his life, lying. The conversations at the lake house about Sam's suspicions went unsaid.

For the longest time, there was silence as Rachel studied his face. He kept eye contact as he knew he must and when she finally looked down at her hands, it was clear to him that she thought he knew far more than he was telling her. When she looked back up at him, her face was a mask. "It's time for me to go, Will."

Months later, he would ask himself why he had lied and lost the trust of his best friend's daughter in her hour of

45

devastation. Only at the very end, when it was far too late, would he finally understand why. And allow himself the certainty that, on that lonely night in that lonely restaurant, he had been right to do so.

CHAPTER TEN
AT THE HOUSE

Alex Kennedy, Will Bennett, and Rachel Greenberg met the homicide detectives the next morning at 9 a.m. in front of the Greenberg house. Rachel, Will and Alex had met for breakfast mostly to reacquaint the two women and to talk about the day ahead. Will recognized right away a change in Rachel, a sense of coolness that was almost icy towards him and only slightly better towards Alex. They'd then gone to the house where the yellow police tape still signaled it a crime scene. It was a dreary November Northern Virginia day with rain in the clouds and a wet chill in the air. The police tape only added to the depression of the day. The neighborhood was as Will remembered it; tree lined and suburban quiet, an urban oasis for the government warriors who toiled each weekday in the nation's capitol and returned each night to be home with family. An oasis now shattered by murder.

The detectives were already there parked in front in their "unmarked" car, dark blue, black walls, and several antennae sprouting from the top and rear of the car. Unmarked my ass, Will thought. The two detectives got out of their car and introduced themselves. Detective Sergeant Robert (don't call me Bob they would soon learn) Davison was about Kennedy's and Bennett's age, trim, and suitably subdued for the occasion. He was polite without being condescending, deferential without being smarmy, and clearly a consummate professional. The judge in Alexandra Kennedy liked him immediately. The lawyer and best friend of Sam Greenberg was not so sure and thought him to be somebody to be very careful of. Davison's partner was a burly younger man who introduced himself as Detective Lonnie Olstrom. Both Kennedy and Bennett would later compare notes and be pleased that they had both determined this was a good cop – bad cop partnership but only because Davison clearly was a good cop and Olstrom was simply Olstrom. Not so good. They wondered aloud later how the two had been put together as a team and came to the conclusion that Davison was just simply unlucky. But unlucky or not, he was also clearly very bright and they would learn as the weeks and months went on, not a nine to five homicide detective.

After the intros, Sergeant Davison, clearly in charge, led them up the front steps. Bennett had been to the house any number of times and had always thought it an old person's home built in the '60s when brick ranches were all the rage and, to his way of thinking, always for old people. It had been affordable when the Greenbergs had bought it years ago and it had served them well over the years. It was, on this gray day, overwhelmingly dark. He sought warmth walking next to his wife. Rachel Greenberg was calm and quiet as she walked up the steps but tears were still so very close to the surface.

Davison took a key out of his pocket and opened the front door. Almost as a courtesy to Rachel, the two detectives went in first, then Rachel, then Judge Kennedy, and finally the lawyer. Rachel had told them at breakfast that particularly Detective Olstrom had been reluctant to include Kennedy and Bennett in at least the initial trip to the home but had relented when it became clear that Rachel was very much on her own and very much needed Will Bennett. But that was before last night and dinner and the stare down and the lie.

Kennedy's first impression on entering the house was that there was almost no air to breathe. Somehow, between Sharon's murder, the number of people who had been involved in the crime scene investigation, the chill of the November morning, and the closing down of the house until just now had simply sucked the oxygen out of the house. She took a moment to get her bearings, took a deep breath thankful for the front door still open for the fresh air, and looked around. It was scary. She knew dozens of people had been through the house combing every inch of it for evidence. But nothing looked out of place. No markings to suggest furniture had been moved; no mess of papers gathered; no muddy footprints in the carpet; nothing. From her vantage point, it was as though time had simply stood still how ever many hours ago when a life had ended in a bedroom.

49

The layout of the house was simple. The group was standing in the gray slate foyer that opened into the living room on the right and formal dining room to the left. Behind it was the kitchen that the Greenbergs had renovated some years back to include an island with bar stools. Behind the living room was a door into the den with a large screen television and leather furniture where most of life was led. A door off the living room to the right led to three bedrooms and two baths, one a master bath off the back master bedroom and the other between two other smaller bedrooms off the same hallway. Rachel's bedroom was in the front of the house and the middle bedroom had been kept for a second child that never came.

Stairs off the foyer led to a finished basement that had two guest rooms, a third bath and a "family room" that was seldom used but always immaculately maintained.

The detectives warned the three visitors that nothing was to be touched. Will immediately went to the kitchen dreading seeing the bedroom. Rachel immediately went to her mother's and father's room, and Kennedy and the detectives stayed right where they were standing in the living room. Finding no clues to absolve his friend and identify the murderer at least in the kitchen but almost overcome with the pictures of a family of three growing up in various stages of the journeys of life, Will pulled himself away, went by the two detectives and his wife, and started through the living room to join Rachel in her parents' bedroom.

Rachel was being held up by the door jamb as she looked in the room. Sheets, covers, mattress, box spring all missing, no doubt at the crime lab. Only the skeleton head and foot board held together by the rails remained. Incredibly little else appeared to have changed. Bennett took it all in, finding he was breathing so shallowly he was getting a little dizzy. A deep breath, a moment to compose, and then his arm around his god daughter. "I am so, so sorry, Rach," he whispered, almost more to himself than to her. She looked up at him with a mask of rage that stunned and scared the hell out of him. "He killed her, he killed her, he killed her. My fucking father killed her!" He had never heard a "damn" come out of her mouth, much less this.

"Whoa girl, we don't know anything like that. And you know your dad wouldn't hurt anybody, you know that."

"He killed her. And you know it." Screaming now, she turned away throwing his arm off her and ran down the hall to her own room. A slam of her door and silence.

Still in shock, Will stood in the door. At first, nothing registered in the room and then slowly his senses returned and he looked with more interest at what was left of the Greenberg's bedroom. The empty space where the mattress and box spring had been, the two reading chairs over by the

51

bay window with the table and light, the open door to the master bath.

Alex at his side, her hand sliding into his. "What the hell?" she whispered.

"Rachel has decided that her father killed her mother and that I know all about it," There was an edge in Bennett's voice she recognized, a quiet anger at the seeming injustice of her dad having done everything for her and for his wife and now being called a killer. Not to mention thinking her god father was an accomplice.

They stood silently for a moment and then went into the room. It had all of the appearances of a room emptied that morning with the hustle and bustle of another busy day ahead for Sam and Sharon. There was a pair of Sam's dress pants on one of the chairs, a discarded dress shirt on top of it, underwear and socks on top of them. Will looked in the bathroom and saw Sam's shaving gear and Dopp kit's contents strewn on the sink. All the picture of normalcy.

Except it wasn't. And it hit Will hard enough to take his breath away. Because in the thirty plus years Bennett had known Sam Greenberg, he would never ever have left a pair of pants and shirt and underwear on a chair and never ever would have left his shaving stuff out. Simply never. The Dopp kit was maybe the cops looking through it, but the pants and shirt and underwear? No way. He stood in the door of the bathroom and looked around. There was something else not quite right. Shower, stool, towels in the rack, then back to the vanity and Sam's Dopp kit. Bennett knew something was a half bubble off plumb or maybe it was just him and this horror and this morning. He turned away from the bathroom, took one more look at the clothes on the chair and walked out.

CHAPTER ELEVEN
THE SIT DOWN

Before Will and Alex had the chance to talk, Rachel was out of her bedroom with a bag of clothes and memory stuff from her room that she wanted out of the house. Life would go on for all of them and, clearly, Rachel wanted as little to do with this house as possible, once a haven and now only a nightmare. She walked into the living room where the detectives had found places to sit.

Sergeant Davison waited for Kennedy and Bennett to bring all of them up to speed on the police investigation. Will and Alex joined the trio.

"I will be straight up with all three of you," Davison began. "Not because either Judge Kennedy, with all due respect to the judiciary, or Mr. Bennett have any role in this but, Rachel, because you asked that they be a part of it." Rachel's face pinched as though she'd eaten a lemon. But Davison was looking squarely at Bennett when he said it and Bennett again thought that Davison was a very formidable guy. Will remembered the misinformation he'd given Rachel about the lake house. Good thing. Sam would be as good as convicted if he wasn't already.

"Preliminary results are back on the autopsy and the gun. Your mom was killed with a single shot to her chest, no signs of external trauma or evidence of a fight, all signs pointing to her knowing the killer. She was found sitting up in bed with pillows behind her as though resting or reading before getting up for the day."

Another pause. "The gun was a Glock 9mm. Most popular among the cops and, because of that, best seller for the public at the moment." Davison paused again, this time from Bennett's perspective, enjoying the moment. "We ran gun shops in the area. Six weeks ago, Sam Greenberg bought a Glock 9 from the Golden Bullet Guns and Ammo Shop over on Jefferson. Passed the background check with no problem and, according to the application, a first time gun owner." Another pause as the detective looked first at Rachel and then at Will. "Either of you know why he wanted a gun?"

Very quietly spoken and very, very serious.

There is silence and then there is silence, sometimes so deep and so profound that you simply have to get through it. Like when the doctor says the cancer has come back and there's nothing more to do, or your wife says she's leaving for another man because she hasn't loved you for years, or a jury comes back with a verdict you never saw coming. That is truly silence. Will Bennett had been through all of those. And they were nothing like this.

"We don't have the weapon but we've been over the house a dozen times and there is no gun here." He didn't need to point out there was also no Sam Greenberg anywhere.

55

Olstrom was chapter two. "As to your dad, we don't have any leads yet but we're just getting started. Airports, trains, busses, nothing. Wallet still here, no sign of credit card use, no contact with his office, no telephone contacts at his office or with known friends." The detective looked at Bennett a second longer than need be. "For now, we think him to be a very important 'person of interest' but no clear idea of where he is." Olstrom stopped to take a breath. As did Bennett. If Sam wasn't dead, at least the cops didn't know where he was either. Looking right at Rachel, it was now Davison's turn. "We think your dad killed your mom. We can't prove it, we don't know why and we hope to God we're wrong. But you need to hear that."

Another awful silence. And then the bombshell. "I know he killed her. She called me three nights ago crying and crying. So not mom. She said my dad was getting worse and worse. Headaches all the time, never sleeping, yelling at her, scaring her, accusing her of cheating on him. My mom would never do that. She was scared to death." Rachel was crying. "She said she thought he was going to kill her. I told her that was silly and we talked for a long time until she got quiet. And when we finally said goodbye, she said 'I love you, Rachel Sarah. No matter what happens, know that.' And she hung up. For the last time."

Hysterical now, somehow her face in Alex's shoulder. "She only called me Rachel Sarah one other time, the time when I told her I was pregnant."

Again the silence so profound that it was deafening.

CHAPTER TWELVE
HISTORY

The five of them there for what seemed like forever. Rarely at a loss as to what to say, Will Bennett was numb. Alexandra Kennedy, also rarely at a loss for words, knew better than to say anything. Rachel Greenberg, after her outburst, seemed almost as though she'd stunned herself into silence. And the two detectives let it play out a little longer.

Finally Olstrom. "When did all that start, Rachel?" Quietly. Maybe not so good yet but willing to pick up some pointers from the master sitting next to him. If there were any doubt that Rachel Greenberg had come to the conclusion that her father had killed her mother, the next twenty minutes forever put that notion to rest.

"All of my life for as long as I've been able to know, there's been a tension between the two of them. One minute kissing and hugging, the next screaming at each other. What about? Anything and everything. Her not working, him working too hard, me, them, not being able to have another kid, what's for dinner, who's cleanin' up. Wasn't like they didn't love each other, just seemed like a part of who they were. After awhile, it became so much a part of what life was like, I guess I thought it was like all families." She stopped almost to catch her breath.

Olstrom again. "Threats, physical stuff, anything like that?"

"Never that I knew about. They'd scream at each other, a couple of times a slammed door, and that was about it." "Cops ever called?" "No, never…"

"What else, Rachel?" She thought for a minute and went on.

"The hardest parts were when he was stressed about something. I know he worried a lot about money and whether there was enough for them and me going to private school and then college, whether he could ever retire." A side look at Bennett.

In his head, game face on, Bennett's eyes rolled back. Sam Greenberg to a T, always worrying about something, always stressing. Inwardly, Bennett flashed to the time Sam had told him he wanted "I told you so" on his tombstone.

"When was the last time that happened?" Davison now.

"That was what was going on. A few weeks ago, mom called to say dad was having really bad headaches. He was spending a lot of time at home in bed, curtains drawn. Going to doctors, getting tests, but mom said there was nothing wrong, just another one of Dad's 'issues' she called them. I could hear it in her voice. She was pissed and just tired of it."

Davison. "Ever any counseling?" "Nope." "Think one of them was fooling around?" A longer pause than Bennett certainly would have liked. "My mom? Absolutely not. She would NEVER do that, never ever." That left a rather large void.

"Dad?" Now there's a softball, Kennedy thought to herself.

"Maybe," a smaller voice now. "He was gone so much. Some times every week. Mom had gained some weight, let herself go, he was a handsome guy. I'd walk down the street with him and see women look at him. So maybe."

This goes any better, we'll have him on death row by noon, Bennett noting they were closing in on 11 a.m. A dozen times, the lawyer in him wanted to interrupt, to defend, to do anything. But for now the silence thing was working. There was nothing to say that was going to make this train wreck any smoother. He looked at his wife a couple of times for a little moral support but her game face never changed.

"Any idea where he's at?" Olstrom, captain of the King's English.

Rachel Greenberg looked right at Wilson Bennett. And so did everybody else. "Whenever he was in trouble, he'd go to Will's place in Michigan."

She was starting to piss him off. First, she says her dad kills her mom, then she tells them why, then she decides he's at his place.

"He was there last week."

Bennett would swear to Alex later that he saw her game face change just enough to see the beginning of what he could only call an 'I told you so smirk'.

CHAPTER THIRTEEN
QUESTIONS

The balloon over Bennett's head looked something like this. Sharon Greenberg was dead, shot once with a 9mm Glock, his best friend having just bought a 9mm Glock for reasons unknown and unsaid, his friend having disappeared without a trace but whose daughter said he always runs to the lake house, the marriage was in trouble…oh…and Sharon Greenberg dead. And last week Sam had been at the lake house pretty certain his wife was having an affair…losing weight, working out.

He glanced at his wife. Now clearly a smirk, sympathetic maybe, but clearly a smirk. Four sets of eyes turned to him. At least she could have looked someplace else. In their early years, she had said once that an honest man needed no memory. He was trying like hell to remember what he'd told Rachel the night before about last week in Michigan and hoped his memory would hold.

And so The Lie, chapter two. Bennett talked about the headaches, the stress Sam had been under at work, the normal frustrations of life, the walks on the beach, the long talks, the tennis, the bike rides, the golf, the seeming return of self confidence and sense of mission to return to normalcy, Sharon's impatience but continued commitment to their love and marriage, talk of the future, talk of the families, talk of the history of the friendship. He finally ran out of steam and looked around the "courtroom" to see how this one had gone. Bennett was not by nature a bullshitter. Four out of five either for sure knew he was bullshitting or had a damn good suspicion. Davison was holding judgment but was leaning towards bullshitting, Olstrom knew Bennett was a lawyer and, therefore, by his definition, was a bullshitter, and Rachel, having had Will confirm what he'd said just last night, was just as certain he was lying. Alex knew the truth. And so did Will.

There were questions about his relationship with Sam, questions about Bennett's knowledge of the marriage, the gun, Sam's disappearance, questions, questions, questions, and then some more, and it was abundantly clear that, while Will was not a "person of interest", his friendship with Sam Greenberg was clearly a major avenue of information for the detectives. Will and Alex would get back to New Mexico but it was clear this was not the end of the story. They wanted to know where he was. Bennett didn't have a clue.

Now after 1 P.M., Olstrom and Davison announced that they had to be back at the station, Rachel was to meet with the people at the funeral home to put the final touches on the service tomorrow, and Will desperately needed to be with his partner.

A last question. "Mind if we have the State Police in Michigan check out the lake house?" Bennett knew it was coming, had tried to think about the right thing to do, knew if he said 'no', there'd be a search warrant issued in Michigan in a heart beat, and said: "Of course not. When do they want to go?" An hour ago would've been perfect, Davison thought but considering the funeral for Sharon Greenberg was tomorrow, the best friend was married to a judge, the knowledge that state troopers would monitor access to the house, led Davison to this.

"Sunday?"

Will nodded and the party broke up.

CHAPTER FOURTEEN
THE LEVAYAH

After Rachel left for the funeral home and the detectives left in the unmarked marked police car, Alex and Will were suddenly alone with the emptiness of the day. Rachel had insisted on driving her own car to the house and it was clear to Kennedy and Bennett that she had put them in her father's camp and that, therefore, for the foreseeable future, she was putting some major distance between them. Will had asked about going to the Temple and even serving a stint as a Shomer for Sharon's body until the Levayah on Saturday. That was politely and firmly refused. Joining her at the Temple for Shabatt that Friday evening was clearly out of the question. So here they were.

The twosome drove into the city for a late lunch at the Tune In, one of the old Capitol Hill restaurants that had been there since Will's law school days. Mostly quiet, content with each other and their own thoughts, they finished lunch and then walked the distance of the Mall holding hands and tourist gazing the sights. Long moments at the Vietnam Wall where both found the names of the few they knew who hadn't come back. Both of them in their own lives had hated that war. Both, years before they had met, had marched against the Vietnam War on the same day in this very city. Alex had been gassed, arrested, and spent some very uncomfortable hours in the stadium detention center. Will, brand new to law school, had worn a yellow arm band marked "Legal" that had given him a modicum of safety. It was one of the strange coincidences of the confluent journeys of their lives, both there, both involved, and only later to connect. Now they raged against the insanity of war and did what they could to make their voices heard.

Little by little they had come to peace with a world that wouldn't, couldn't change in their lifetimes. But they could still rant from time to time. And surely did.

On the way back, Alex turned to Will. "So where is he? Lake house? On the run? Dead?" The last spoken knowing it had been on her husband's mind since Wednesday.

"I have not a fucking clue, Alex, not a fucking clue. If he got to the lake house, he's about to be very screwed. He can't be on the run, where would he go and what's he using? No car, no cards, no wallet, no money. Besides you know him as well as me, guy needs a map to get to work every day."

She wouldn't let it go. "So dead is what's left?"

"Something's wrong, Alex. I can feel it. The gun, the disappearing, the shooting, the clothes in the room, the bathroom mess, none of it makes any sense. He would never buy a gun, he hated them as much as me. He would never disappear, he doesn't know how to do that. And the clothes? You kidding? Never would Sam Greenberg leave a pair of his underwear on a chair. Never." Bennett's mind noodled on something else, that nagging feeling he'd had at the house. Couldn't get it to rise to the surface and left it.

"OK, how about this? Robber breaks in, surprises Sam and Sharon, kills Sharon and kidnaps Sam thinking he'll ask for a ransom?" Alex.

"Nothing is gone. Sharon is lying in bed looking like she clearly knows the shooter, no evidence of a struggle. No call for ransom. And the goddamn underwear on the chair." Will.

"OK OK. Sam bought the gun because he thought she was fooling around, confronted her with it that morning, she confessed, and he killed her with the Glock and is now on the run, probably still here in the area. Maybe he just didn't get it all thought through." Alex.

And here was the worst part. It was what made the most sense.

They went back to the "Palace on First", as they now referred to it, in the very late afternoon with bags of what were traditionally their New Year's feast. Two bottles of champagne (one would do but they both thought they might need a spare on this trip); cheeses and crackers; grapes; oysters for Will, anchovies for Alex; a loaf of sourdough bread. And thou.

Early to bed but not to sleep for quite some time. Amazing what a little stress can do when it gets channeled in the right direction. The only problem with getting to bed that early is that waking up comes sooner than it should for most normal folk. So…at 4:30 the next morning, they were up, in their sweats, and off to find a 24 hour diner.

They found Sophie's 24 Hour Eats downtown and took comfort in the presence of police cars and pick up trucks. A locals' place. Two calendars on the wall, waitresses who clearly had spent the better part of their lives doing exactly what they were doing now, and omelets and home fries to die for. Alex and Will consciously avoided talking about the elephant long enough to get fed, read the Washington Post, and take in the local color. With still hours to go when they finished, they drove into northern Virginia for what Will thought would be time in the country to calm them down. Things had changed.

Expressways that were six lanes wide, cars and trucks at warp speed even on an early chilly November Saturday and box houses, condos and apartment complexes as far as the eye could see. And a super mall every other exit. Back to the "Palace" to shower and dress and early to the Temple.

Will had been there on a number of occasions over the years with Sam and his family and had met many of the members of the Temple. But this day would be very different.

News by whatever means had traveled fast and, from the very minute Will and Alex walked in, they were met with a coldness that was stunning. Friends of the Greenbergs' that Will had known since law school days turned away when they saw him coming. They went in and sat down and clearly were a crowd of two with several seats separating them from the rest of the congregation.

Bennett would later remember almost nothing of the service other than it was very long and very sad. His thoughts were on Sam and the nightmare that was now a part of all of their lives. He tried to make sense of being shunned by people he knew and whose grief he shared. Startling but not altogether unexpected. He was, after all, Sam's best friend and had been for 30 years. The Greenbergs' friends clearly had come to the conclusion that Sam had killed Sharon and was on the run. It certainly made sense to this group and understandably so. But Will Bennett knew differently, he knew it in his heart and in his soul. He just didn't know what to do about it.

At the close of the service, the congregation was invited to a lunch in the basement of the Temple. Will and Alex were torn about whether to join the mourners or make a run for it. As they followed people out of the sanctuary, they ran into Davison and Olstrom who pulled them aside.

Olstrom. "I spoke with the Michigan Staties and they'll be at your place tomorrow. Need to know directions and how to get in. And whether you're going to be there." Off balance, Bennett gave the directions to Olstrom who dutifully wrote them down, told the detectives where the key was, and hesitated for a moment about whether to try to get there, mentally trying to remember how badly they had left the place and what the chances were that Sam was indeed there and what Bennett could do even if he were there. Finally, "No need. Tell them to leave it the way they find it."

Alex spoke. "Gentlemen, Will and I are heading back to Albuquerque today or tomorrow. Any need for us to stay?" Now it was Davison who seemed unsettled. "Why so quick to leave?" Having apparently missed the widening chasm between Will and Alex and Rachel and the rest of the congregation, Davison had thought the two would stick around for moral support for Rachel or to see if Sam Greenberg turned up.

"Nothing more we can do here," Alex said trying to close off a line of conversation before it got started. Davison paused for another moment, glanced at Olstrom and said that he knew where to find them and that they'd keep them posted on developments including the State Police visit to the lake house. They parted, Davison and Olstrom leaving the Temple and Will and Alex going to the lunch in the basement. Both felt the same coldness when they walked in and a joint silent executive decision to beat feet was made. A perfunctory 'we'll be in touch' hug with Rachel that was barely acknowledged and Alex and Will almost sprinted from the gathering, Alex's cell phone was on speed dial to get them home.

A lucky connection late out of National through Dallas and the key in the door at the townhouse at 11 p.m.. Will briefly thought of calling the lake house just in case Sam was there but Alex talked him out of it. Too easy to trace, too complicit for comfort. Exhausted emotionally, the two collapsed into their spoon and were asleep in minutes.

CHAPTER FIFTEEN
ALL GONE

The next three days passed for Will Bennett as though he were slogging through the high humidity of a Michigan dog days of August spell. No energy, no appetite, no nothing. Alex Kennedy was back on the bench Monday certainly better off than her husband but not by much. Way too many questions, way too few answers. Olstrom had called Monday afternoon to say the Michigan State Police had found nothing of interest at the lake house other than some samples of Sam Greenberg's DNA from the bathroom. It was hardly earth shaking news given the evidence taken from the house in Alexandria. No calls from Rachel, no calls from Sam.

It was almost dream like in its unreality and Will wondered if maybe he'd wake up and all would be back to normal. Until Wednesday when his direct dial phone rang and Will noted the 703 area code. Virginia. Rachel's cell phone.

"Wilson Bennett. You knew it all the time. Where the hell is my father? Where the hell is he?" Voice rising, nearly incoherent, Rachel Greenberg went through a string of venom aimed at her father that tested even Will's vocabulary. Patience a virtue, he kept silent and finally, she ran out of things to call her dad.

"Rachel?" Tentative, wondering if it really was over. "What are we talking about here, girl?" Calm, stay calm, stay very calm. Quieter now but still very angry. "My father cleaned out every fucking savings and checking account they had. Every one. There is NO money left anywhere. Even cashed out my mom's life insurance. It's all gone, all gone, all gone." Her voice tailed off to almost a whisper. "And you know where he is and you know where the money is, I know you know, Will. And you need to tell me where he is and where the money is. Now." A harsh measured meanness to her voice that was part anger, part desperation, and part pure hatred. "And if you don't tell me right now, my next call is to the police."

A hundred questions went through Bennett's head. How, when, why, where. How had he done it? And why? And how? And he allowed himself a slender thread, a hope that this meant Sam was alive and on the run. And another disquieting thought. He hadn't known Rachel well, had seen her less often than he should have, but never had there been a glimmer of this kind of anger. He shook the thought off in a heartbeat. Mother dead, father vanished and all the money gone. Just a little stress. Just a little.

"Rachel. I know nothing about what you're talking about. Nothing. If you want to talk about it, we need to and I want to but I swear I have no idea what you're talking about."

Rachel Greenberg hung up.

73

Just before lunch in the east, Bennett dialed the number for the Alexandria police, asked for homicide, and then for Detective Sergeant Davison. A long pause and finally: "Detective Sergeant Davison." Very stern, very cool, very professional.

Two can play that game. "Detective Sergeant, Wilson Bennett here in Albuquerque. I just got off the phone with Rachel Greenberg and she tells me that the Greenberg's financial accounts have all been emptied. Is that true?"

Bennett could almost see the wheels turn back in Virginia. Bennett had no right to know anything about the investigation and Davison's first instinct was to tell him to pound sand especially because if Bennett were lying about what he knew about Sam Greenberg's disappearance, he already knew the accounts were cleaned out. On the other hand, Lonnie Olstrom had told Rachel Greenberg without authorization; and if Bennett didn't know, maybe he could help, and, either way, who cared about a breach in police protocol? Sharon Greenberg dead, Sam missing, and Rachel already knew. Davison needed an arrest.

"Starting about six months ago, Greenberg began to make periodic withdrawals…big withdrawals…from every account the couple had. Day to day checking he pretty much left alone but there was a money market account that over three months dropped to zero; a savings account the same thing; some major stocks and mutual funds sold on his order; and finally thirteen days ago, he cashed in his wife's whole life policy."

Bennett. "How much?"

Davison. "All told, about two and a half million."

"What's left?"

"About 3 thou in the checking and that's it. But here's a weird thing. Rachel's tuition, room and board and everything was paid for the whole first year. What crazy man does that?"

"Who told you that?" Bennett asked, the puzzlement in his voice.

"Rachel. For some reason she had checked with UVA's Finance Office and they confirmed it."

So there's the one good thing, Will thought to himself. "So what happened?"

"Substance, a verrry expensive girlfriend, gambling. We're trying to run down all three. Care to help out on any of those options?"

Bennett mulled it over. Helping homicide detectives try to prove his best friend was the killer was not something he was particularly interested in doing. But his friend was missing, there were questions that he couldn't answer, and 2000 miles away, his only possible ally was Davison. Bennett thought about what he should do, what Alex would do, and came to a decision.

CHAPTER SIXTEEN
A BEAUTIFUL FRIENDSHIP BEGINNING

"In the first years after law school," Bennett started, "Sam used to fool around with small time gambling. Pro football, basketball. Never college, never horses, just piddly stuff. I remember one time being in DC seeing him and stopping at a jewelry store downtown on K St so he could drop off a payment. Nickels, dimes and dollars. Nothing more. A few years later after he and Sharon were married, I asked him about it and he said he'd quit. Thought it was stupid." He could hear Davison's fingers on the keyboard.

"Substance? Girlfriend? Understand your friend was quite the stud when he was younger." Geez, they were working this case hard. OK OK, Sam'd been a player when he was younger and he used to piss Bennett off big time. They'd walk into bars, the tall swarthy handsome guy from New York City and the little pastie guy with the flannel shirt from Michigan. Guess who'd win that contest? And there was that fling Sam had had with Susie Barker, the beautiful young woman Bennett had pined for, that had almost killed the relationship but didn't. But that was a long ago story. Back to now. Because, as far as he knew, Greenberg had been faithful to Sharon. There had never been a suggestion otherwise and Will, of anyone would have known.

"As far as I know, Detective Sergeant…" "Call me Robert, Mr. Bennett". "Then call me Will…please. As far as I know, Sam was faithful to Sharon. He traveled a lot, met a lot of different people, got to be in glamorous places, but I never once heard him talk about anybody other than Sharon."

"Ever ask him?"

"Robert, I'm a guy. Sex is what we think about. What we talk about. Of course I asked him." Will thought he heard a quiet chuckle over the phone.

"Would he be straight with you?"

Will thought of all the things the two of them talked about over the years, knew the deep level of non-judgmental trust that was their strongest bond, and said, "I can't imagine he wouldn't have. Can't imagine."

"Substance?"

"No way. Sam would have one drink and begin to speak in tongues. Drugs? We smoked some dope in law school when one of us could afford it but especially after Rachel, I don't think so."

Almost kindly, Davison asked another question quieter this time. "I suppose another option was that Mr. Greenberg was bleeding the accounts knowing, months ago, he was going to kill his wife and make a run for it?" Silence long enough for Will to understand it was a question.

Will's first thought was to laugh but he held it. There was something about this phone call that rang true and he didn't want to fuck it up. Because in the time ahead, he would need Davison a lot more than Davison would need him. Even if Davison didn't quite understand that yet.

"I don't think so, Robert." Will paused. "I just don't see it."

The wrap up. "Of all the options, gambling?"

"He dabbled twenty-five years ago, that's all I know." Helpful.

"You think Sharon Greenberg was having an affair?" Even quieter.

Jesus Christ, who is this guy? Will tried to remember the details of what he now thought of as The Lie that he had told Rachel and again balanced loyalty to his friend and trying to protect him from giving the police an age old motive with wanting so desperately to know what happened.

"When we were at the lake, Sam broached it. Said Sharon was upset about what he was going through, she was losing weight, working out, but I know…knew Sharon…and that wasn't her style. She could be crazy making but she loved him and was loyal. Don't think so."

A few more questions about the lake house conversations that Will hoped were consistent and finally this.

"Will. Olstrom and I are absolutely convinced that Sam Greenberg killed his wife and is on the run. We're not sure why yet but he is No. 1 on our list. And he's gone missing. Taking the money over months leads to gambling, first, then a girl friend, and then maybe just wanting to make a run for it. Shit, we all think those thoughts from time to time. So we think he did it and, if he's still alive, we'll find him.

For reasons that Lonnie Olstrom will never ever understand, I believe you and I think you're telling me the truth, at least about the important things. I think if you knew where he was, you'd tell me. Do I think you know more about him than you're telling me, bet your ass." A very long pause that Will chose not to fill.

"But if this were my friend, I'd do exactly what you're doing. So here's the deal I want to make with you. I'll call you at least once a week and tell you some of what we're doing. Probably not all but the high points. In return, if you hear from him, even if you don't tell me where he is, I want you to promise that you'll do everything you can to make him come in.

Fair?"

"Fair."

"Goodbye Will."

"Goodbye Robert."

Will Bennett sat in his office and chewed on the call. He's a cop for Christ's sake, of course he's going to try to get under your skin. He wants Sam Greenberg in the worst way. Will could only imagine the pressure on him to find Greenberg and arrest him. So why not screw with Greenberg's best friend and use him every which way? Which is what I'd do for sure if I were him. But then why all the volunteered information?"

He had a headache. And reached for the phone to see if Alex could take an early lunch/brunch.

CHAPTER SEVENTEEN
AS TIME GOES BY

Months later, Will would try to explain what the next weeks were like. Life would seem normal for little stretches and then there would be times of overwhelming sadness and aloneness. It was the uncertainty of it all that was so hard, the lack of closure, the lack of finality. He talked endlessly with Alex about it but, after awhile, there was nothing that could be said that hadn't already been said. She was patient, compassionate and nurturing but, after awhile, there was nothing left.

Even their sex life drifted for awhile, Will with less interest as a part of the grayness of his world. And that was something Alexandra Kennedy would not tolerate. A weekend away to the Inn at Cloudcroft in southern New Mexico, well stocked with the Viagra emergency supply, some Plymouth English Gin and some Jameson's, and by the end of the weekend that part of their lives was back on track. Kennedy marveled at the consistency of that relationship. In the years before Will Bennett, she had never been able to sustain a sexual relationship more than at best a year or two. Men never quite got it, she thought, and finding someone who actually liked to please her past his own pleasure was a difficult task. Then there was having to put up with the drooling, body odor, stale beer breath and it wasn't very long before she was on to something else. Her best friend once described her exes as "road kill on the highway of lust" and when Will had come along, the odds were long against this one lasting any longer than the rest.

But it had. And that had surprised friends and colleagues and mostly Alex. She used to wonder about what made this one so different so far down the highway. But trying to figure out what felt so good seemed contrary and she let it go, simply chalking it up to "chemistry." Still there after all the years.

Detective Sergeant Robert Davison remained true to his word. He called every week even if there was only the mundane to report. Alexandria homicide had become convinced that Sam Greenberg had a gambling addiction that had gotten him way over his head and that that was the reason for the withdrawals wiping out the Greenberg assets. But it was mostly because they had ruled out substance and/or a girl friend. They could find no direct evidence connecting Sam to gambling or gamblers but opined that that wasn't especially surprising if his best friend didn't know. Davison and Olstrom tested a new theory. Sharon Greenberg had been killed because Greenberg owed way too much to somebody. Common stuff for big time gamblers. Except neither Greenberg nor the gun had turned up.

So Greenberg was still on the A list for the detectives. Are you kidding? He was the A list. And nobody could find any trace of him. In a way, it helped the gambling connection and the theory that both of them had been killed after whoever it was had gotten everything they could. But finding the bodies was the message. Finding one and not the other made no sense. So he was still No. 1.

But it still didn't explain the pants and shirt and the underwear on the chair and the Dopp kit in disarray in the bathroom. And that something else that still hovered in Will's consciousness. Will hung on to that something else even as Alex Kennedy, over time, discounted it to zero.

Why? Because it was all he had.

Time went by. And the rhythm of life returned to Alex and Will. There was always the cloud of the unknown but they were hardly the first friends or family who had struggled with that. Will's practice continued to prosper even when he didn't much care whether it did or not; Judge Kennedy continued to survive the Zoo Days, tried the felonies and a smattering of civil cases, and the two of them continued their love affair. As with all tragedies, they had lost a step but there were even times when Will could forget about the events of the last fall. They spent a long weekend at the lake house in early April and that was at first very hard. Pictures on the fridge, a left over chardonnay bottle half full, a tooth brush that could only have been Sam's in the downstairs bathroom. How did the Staties miss it?

But after all, it was the lake house and a fire in the wood stove and some walks on the beach helped. They talked about growing old, about life, the wonder of Lake Michigan, the beauty of the woods. In the comfort of each other. And the love making returned to its proper place at the Inn at Cloudcroft after all the distractions. What's the deal with these old folks? The glue that had held them through the toughest of times, after all the years, held true.

Through it all and because of it all, Alex and Will grew even closer. Couples, hell, all relationships, get good times and bad times and what relationships do with the bad times defines them. Sharon's murder, Sam's disappearance, no answers to so many questions only seemed to strengthen them. Us against the world. And it worked.

One night on the patio in the Old Town townhouse, the two of them got to talking about baggage and how the older you got, the more you shed. And so you could take on new stuff. Like parents getting old or you getting old or kids never quite separating themselves from the home nest. Or a world in constant turmoil. Or a best friend already convicted in most circles of killing his wife and gone missing. Or whatever. But in the gray to black, there was some light. And it was clean.

Still, Will missed his best friend. They had always been there for each other. They had talked about a time when one of them was gone and the other not and how each of them hoped, within certain parameters, like each getting to be a 100 and still in perfect health, they would be the first to go. And here it was but different. Because Sam wasn't gone, only seriously MIA. No end, no closure.

Even still as the days went by, the acuteness of the loss and sadness and pain warmed to the memories of days gone by. He was there always and forever and life moved on. Rachel? A distant memory. No contact even though Will had left messages. He kept up to date on her through Robert Davison. She had finished her first year at UVA, straight As, a hardship scholarship for her sophomore year, still hating her father with Will not far behind.

Mid June. The monsoon season in Albuquerque. Will was on his way out the door to depositions and the phone rang.

"Will? Robert. I have some news. I think you need to come here."

Bennett paused. "Why? What?"

"Couple of things I think you can help with. Know anybody named Sy?"

Wilson thought for a minute. "There's a Sy Silver that was a good friend of the Greenbergs. Only one I can think of. Why?"

"Rachel was going through a safe deposit box with the bank officer and found some letters from somebody named Sy to Sharon. Started around a year and a half before the murder, last one last October." Davison paused for effect. "Nothing real specific but more than couples' friends and she saved them."

Bennett thought for a moment. Sy Silver? Okay looking boring corporate type, getting bald sooner than he should? Was he at the funeral? At best a stretch.

"Anything else, Robert?"

There was clearly one more thing on Davison's mind and, even though they were 2,000 miles apart, Will had come to know this Detective Sergeant well enough to know the other shoe was about to drop.

"I've been thinking all morning how to say this without sounding completely crazy."

Will let the silence linger.

Davison sighed. "I'm not so certain Sam Greenberg killed his wife."

More silence. Then, "Why? You've been pretty sure so far."

"I know. And Olstrom and the Chief both think I've gone soft. But this thing with the letters and now the possible gambling connection. And even wiping out the accounts. Everybody I've talked to, everybody, has talked about how devoted Greenberg was to Rachel. They waffle on the marriage, on his job, on him as a friend, but never on Rachel. Would he really leave her high and dry? Kill her mother and take the money and run? Just doesn't feel quite right."

For Davison, that was a speech. And Bennett could tell that this case continued to haunt the Detective Sergeant even all the cold months later.

"How can I help, Robert?"

"Will, I honestly don't know for sure. Maybe it's nothing more than moral support. But I've been thinking it might be kind of fun if you were the one to confront Sy Silver. Wear a wire. Be a deputy detective. Even get you a plastic badge."

"Right. And a gun?"

"Sure. Plastic of course." Will could hear a touch of playfulness in Davison's voice.

"When do you want me?"

"When can you get here?"

CHAPTER EIGHTEEN
BACK TO THE BEGINNING

Rarely at a loss for words, the Honorable Alexandra Kennedy leaned back in her chair stunned for a moment. Then, "What the fuck!" The picture of decorum on the bench and in public life, Alex Kennedy was not above the profane in private.

"What the fuck. So let me get this right. Your new best friend, Detective Sergeant Davison, wants you to leave Albuquerque, fly halfway across the country, and be the one to confront somebody you really don't know very well at all and accuse him of having an affair with your best friend's wife. And wear a wire. What the fuck."

"You said that a couple of times already."

"Wilson W." Never a good sign. "What is he thinking? Why you? Why not the police? They have anything other than some letters? How bad are they? Sex? Trysts? Assignations…?" The last word drawn out for effect.

Big time trial lawyer. "I never really got specifics. All he said was that they were more than one would write a friend. And she had saved them in a safe deposit box." Will hoped that last piece would help.

"What about the gambling connection? Does he want you to go undercover for that too? Jesus Christ."

They had worked on the issue of sarcasm in their relationship and had jointly agreed it was a bad thing. But there were times that it just couldn't be avoided and, at least in her head, this was one of them. Her husband, off to Alexandria, Virginia, to play at being an undercover cop because Detective Sergeant has intuition? Would that be woman's intuition? Will Bennett was one of the most transparent people she had ever met. He was going to confront somebody who may have been having an affair with his best friend's wife? And then get him to confess that he had killed his lover and framed Sam Greenberg. And without a gun? What the fuck.

She glanced at her watch. "I have to get back on the bench. We'll talk about this tonight." Judicial, cold, not happy. Judge Kennedy stood to put on her robes and Will beat retreat.

Well, that went well, he thought to himself as he left the courthouse and walked back to his office. He'd never say this to her out loud, of course, but there was a certain logic to her thinking. Will Bennett was about as pacifist as one could get and still survive in the wars of the civil justice system. He abhorred conflict in his personal life, abhorred war on any level for any reason, and would have been perfectly fine if the Founding Fathers had never thought to include the Second Amendment in the Bill of Rights. Alexandra Kennedy, on the other hand, had grown up with guns and, as far as Will knew, had three hand guns hidden at the town house. She had promised she'd never tell him where they were and, to date, he had had no interest in finding them.

Still a half block away from emails and phone calls and interrogatories and mail to go through, it dawned on Will that there was a certain danger to this. His recall of Sy Silver was that he was a corporate type lawyer with one of the big firms in DC. His family went to the same Temple as the Greenbergs with kids on either side of Rachel and they had become social friends. Will had met Silver several times on his infrequent trips to Virginia to see Sam and he had sat at the same table with Mr. and Mrs. Silver at Rachel's Bat Mitzvah five years ago. He searched for some defining memory of Sy Silver and the only thing he could come up was a visage of a harmless… lawyer. Nice, conversational but a transactional guy for Christ's sake. Billing north of $800 an hour to clients who would pay it, poring over details of contracts that were mind numbing in their tediousness, and boring to match the work he did. Of course he probably made a million dollars a year and that would help. But the time with the Silvers had only reinforced, once again, Bennett's decision to be a trial lawyer.

An affair with Sharon Greenberg? That would never ever have crossed Will's radar screen in a million years. But

Davison wanted him to come to Alexandria to put it all to the test. And his wife dead set against it.

In the office. "Liz, what do we look like the next several days?"

Uh oh. That tone of voice she knew so well. Her mind went through the rest of the week. This was Tuesday, Wednesday was a lunch with a friend she knew could be moved, Thursday was a day set aside to put together a mediation brief, and Friday was two motions that she could get cover on. "Nothing we can't move as long as you take the Sitterly case with you to do the brief. It's due to the mediator Friday but Monday will probably do. Where are we off to, Will?"

God, he loved this woman. They had been together 12 years starting back in Michigan and when the dreaded moment came when he had told her that he and Alex were getting married and that he was moving to New Mexico, she had taken the news stoically, had waited a day, and then had asked if there were room for her in the move. Kids grown, divorced for several years, tired of Michigan winters, there was little left for her other than two grandsons who she doted on but who were quickly growing out of spending time with their grandmother. Liz understood she needed more in her life than a job and two grandsons. A call by Will to his new firm and the deal was done. She got her house sold and, three months later, joined Will Bennett in Albuquerque.

What had been amazing was how quickly she had come to love the desert and the people of New Mexico. She regained a spark he hadn't seen in her in years. Popular around the office, she had begun dating a man several years younger, had toned up big time and had taken up mountain biking with a passion.

For all of the years the two of them had worked together, they had remained only friends, one of those few female male relationships where sex hadn't gotten in the way of friendship. He had helped her through the roller coaster of a divorce from an abusive, alcoholic asshole and she had been a rock through his own divorce and the ups and downs of his long distance relationship with Alexandra Kennedy.

And here they were.

"Virginia. There's something I need to do." She knew better than to pry.

"When?"

"Tomorrow?" "I'll see what I can do." She was gone only to return in a few minutes. "American out of here on the 8:30 through Dallas and then into National at 3:45. Confirmed on first class Dallas to DC and wait listed from here to there. Open ended for the return. Hertz car. Holiday Inn on First." All business, always professional.

93

And now all he had to do was tell his wife.

CHAPTER NINETEEN
SIX MILES HIGH

Wednesday morning, comfortable in his last minute upgrade to Dallas, the New York Times in his lap, Wilson Bennett reflected on the events of the last 24 hours. The call from Davison, his conversation with Alex, reservations made by Liz, coverage worked out, the call to Davison to tell him he was coming. And then home.

It had not gone well. Alex Kennedy had her virtues but never ending patience was not one of them.

"Wilson W, you have done some of the dumbest things in your day that any human being has a right to do and live. But this takes the cake. It has been ..." she paused to count the months, "...8 months since Sharon was killed and your friend disappeared. You know I'm sorry and you know I know how awful this has been for you. But Jesus, Will, you have got to let this go. If he was still alive and he hadn't done it, don't you think you would have heard from him? Eight months? His best friend?"

The next couple of hours were spent in an ever escalating emotional "conversation" that ranged from never giving up to having to let it go. Will: I will do anything I can for him. Alex: it's what cops are for. And so on. Ending badly. With barely a good bye in the morning. No good bye sex. Driving his own car to the airport. Now, that's cold. On the way out the door, her: "Your flight's guaranteed," quietly, but it was their tradition. He knew she'd be there when he got home.

Been awhile since we've gone that bad, Will thought as American 1568 began the descent into Dallas/Fort Worth. On time, easy walk to the flight to National, and back up into the sky. Neither Alex nor Will had ever figured out how these skinny little aluminum tubes could stay up in the air for so long and why they never simply fell to the ground in a heap. They both knew it had something to do with physics and force and vectors and whatever other bullshit there was to it but it was beyond them. He smiled at the conversations they had had around the topic and kicked himself for not calling her from Dallas. Nice testosterone, Will. Shit.

Then thoughts about the past eight months, renoodling all that had gone on, all of the questions and knowing none of the answers. Will knew why he was going to Virginia to do this. Simply because he had to. If there were anything he could do to put it to bed, he would. He trusted Davison. And if Davison thought he would be of some use, he would be there. Because if things were reversed with Sam...

He closed his eyes and remembered back. It had been 23 years now that Will's dad had gotten sick. Lung cancer and nothing much to do about it. They had found a tumor on the femur too and had operated on it in the hopes of giving him some semblance of a quality of life for what was left of it. But the tumor had been much bigger than they had thought and while his dad had survived the surgery and had survived the radiation, he would be confined to a wheel chair for whatever time was left. His dad had very much wanted to get to Florida where they had retired, away from the cold of the Michigan winter. So the plan had been hatched. Mom and Dad Bennett would fly and Will would drive their car and dog to Florida to pick them up at the airport. Twenty four head start, pushing hard but doable. He had a wrongful death trial starting the following Monday and a need to get home but this trip trumped all.

Sam had called every other day during that time checking on him, a shoulder to cry on when others needed him to be strong. When he found out about the road trip, 24 hours later he was with Will in Michigan helping load the car for the two of them and the dog with the cooler in the back seat packed with beer. A great road trip, successful mission, his folks in Florida for the three months his dad had left. Sam forever.

That was Sam, that was their friendship, and that was why he was on his way to Virginia.

The sharp descent in past the monuments, over the waters of the Potomac, impossibly in safely. No luggage but a desperate sprint to the men's room, no voice mails from the home front, and the call to the Judge.

"She's still on the bench, Will, and for awhile. Want me to pull her?" Karen said. "No thanks Karen. Voice mail is OK."

After the inevitable "You've reached the chambers of..." Will left this: "I'm in DC safe and sound, on my way to the Holiday Inn, and I meet with Davison in the morning. I love you, I love you, I love you. I'm sorry for this and for last night and for everything. But I'm here. Call if you wish. Nope, please call." He hung up.

The Hertz counter, the ride to the lot, and off for what was to be the 20 minute drive to the hotel that took a detour almost by itself to the Greenberg home. He drove slowly by and was devastated by the aloneness of a house that had once been a home. A 'For Sale' sign that had been there long enough for it to have developed a definite lean, an empty bin below the sign for informational flyers that had run out long ago and were not likely to be replaced any time soon, lawn and yard in disarray with nothing done but the most elementary of mowings. Sadness. An incredible sadness that caught him by the throat, let him have some tears in the comfort of the car, a turnaround in the cul-de-sac, then he parked the rental and got out.

Will stretched and allowed himself the emotion of looking at what had been, what he had known, and what would never be again. Still light in June and knowing the neighbors were probably at their windows, he walked up the drive, looked in the windows, only to find nothing had changed. Furniture where it had been, somebody had cleaned the kitchen, almost as it had been that November morning when they had all met at the house. Very fucking spooky. Will Bennett was not prone to chills. But today, chills. And cold.

Time to get to the hotel and a drink and dinner.

On his way to the hotel, his phone rang. Now 7:00 P.M. Eastern time and 5:00 Albuquerque, Judge Kennedy was just getting off the bench. "Will." "Alex." After all the years and tears, the voice that still made him skip a beat.

"So, here's the deal. This is still a stupid thing to do. Truly. But I love you and I always will. If you want me there, I'll cancel the next couple of days and get there. And I'm sorry for last night. And for this morning. And for not taking you to the airport. I'm an asshole. So are you."

A silence. This was about as good an apology as he would ever get from the good judge. He knew it and she knew it. Don't fuck this one up, Will.

"You're right, I'm an asshole and I'm sorry and I think you're right, I'm stupid and here I am and I love you. I won't be here long enough for you to come, stay home, stay the course, and please know I love you more now than ever. I can't wait to get home."

"Come home Will." Soft click of the phone.

A peaceful end to the tumult of the morning, the knowledge she was still willing to wave the pink hankie on the side line even though she still thought him insane. Knowing she'd be there when he got home.

He got to the Holiday Inn, checked in, and called Davison's voice mail at work to call him in the morning. Then something he hadn't done in a long long time. He went to the local liquor store, bought a fifth of Gordon's Gin and a bag of peanuts and went back to the room. A bucket of ice, peanut shells aimed at the waste basket but not always connecting, well into the fifth, the Nationals on TV going down badly. Then nothing.

7:00 a.m. The phone and Davison wanting to meet for breakfast at Sophie's in an hour. Bennett was in that stage of semi-hangover where way too much had been drunk but early enough to bed for a long night's sleep and therefore only the mildest of headaches. But a morning breath that would take most of the morning to get right. "I'll be there."

Will swung his legs out of bed, had some momentary dizziness, and then up. He looked at the shelf where the ice bucket and gin bottle stood a bit like soldiers left standing after the battle. More than half the fifth gone, peanut shells helter skelter in the room, and an overwhelming urgent need to pee and brush his teeth.

In that order.

What was that joke about people who didn't drink? The problem is that when you wake up, it's as good as you're going to feel all day.

To the john and the day ahead.

CHAPTER TWENTY
BREAKFAST

You can go to any state in the country and find a diner that will look almost exactly like Sophie's. Will, not altogether a 100% but close enough, was dressed in blue jeans and his GW T shirt and walked in at promptly 8 a.m. Davison was already in a booth across the way and Will made his way there. There was a handshake and an initial lack of comfort with each other that they both felt. Weeks of talking on the phone and now face to face for the first time since the horror of last November. Will's take was that Davison looked older, a little balder, but much the same as eight months ago. Robert's take was that the months had taken a heavy toll on Bennett, a little thinner but not by much, and far more tired than before, the eyes and the bags under them a dead giveaway.

Will sat down in the booth, picked up the same menu hundreds of diners were offered every morning, and opted for as much grease as a vegetarian could gather. Robert remained quiet as if silence would bridge what the two of them had to get to.

"So. Life. How are you?" Robert asked. Orders given and time to talk.

"Life is OK. Grace is taking a year off and thinking about law school. Alex still moving a million miles a minute, dispensing justice like pills. All told, life is good in the desert. You?" Still on guard, still holding some cards close, waiting for the other side to lay a card down.

A very long pause. Will looked at Davison and saw him, really saw him, maybe for the first time. This was about to go to a depth he hadn't expected. Men are like that, he thought, live most of their lives in a wading pool and every once in a while head for the deep end whether they want to or not. "S'up?" More silence and then.

"Will, Rebecca and I are getting divorced. She comes home about three months ago and tells me it's over. Needs some space. Hardest thing she's ever worked through. Wants the kids to stay with me because I'm the steady Eddie. Wants it to be friendly and peaceful. Loves me but needs to work things out. 'Robert,' she says to me, 'I'm gay.'"

The balloon over Will's head. 'I'm gay?' Yikes, says the balloon. A showstopper. No emotion. Don't show any emotion. Why me?

"How are you, Robert?"

"Day to day, hour to hour. Not in a million years did I think Rebecca was gay. We had a great sex life at least up until the kids, and, even after, satisfactory." A breath. "Satisfactory. So satisfactory, she decided she was gay. Satisfactory." Davison looked at his coffee mug. And then up. "Other than that, about perfect."

103

"Your kids? " Will remembered at least two.

"Robert Jr. is 12, into sports, being OK with it all for the most part. Fran is 10 and struggling. Cries a lot, especially at night, and doesn't understand. But shit, neither do I so I'm not much help. Struggling in school. She's taking the brunt."

"And you, Robert?"

Sergeant Detective Robert Davison took a deep breath, a long drink of coffee, and made a decision. "I'm about as fucked up as a guy can be." Pause. "But I'm going to get through it and so are the kids." Another breath. Quieter. "And so are the kids."

"I'm sorry. I really am." Will knew better than to take sides in something he knew almost nothing about. "I can tell you it will get better because it will. But there's not much to do about the pain in the meantime except be OK with it. But it'll get better."

"Thanks Will."

"Kids know about the gay part?"

"Hard to say. Rebecca sees the kids quite a bit and they talk about her good friend, Alice, who I guess is around a lot but I don't know if they've put it together. And I'm not about to go there." Anger now in his voice.

Maybe it was the openness of the disclosure and maybe it was Will feeling badly for Robert and maybe it was

Robert feeling some empathy of loss and maybe all of it, but the uncomfortable factor disappeared like a sun burning off a morning haze. Because all of a sudden here the two of them were, levels below where either of them thought they would be. Will had lost his best friend and Robert had lost his wife.

"Getting some help?" Will asked.

"Yup. Started with the police shrink but unless you're there because you shot somebody, not much help. So I found a woman who's really been great. All these years, you're a cop trying to help and then something like this goes down and you come to realize how much you've walled off your own self. So turns out there is a lot of shit not very far below the surface that's coming out. But here's the best part."

The food arrived without fanfare or discussion and silence until the waitress reheated coffee and left.

Will waited. "My shrink's gay." Davison laughed and it was real. "Life. Why didn't somebody give us a road map?"

"Cause who'd want to take this trip?"

Davison laughed again. "Maybe. So. On other fronts." Davison pulled a bulky envelope out of his briefcase on the floor and gave it to Will.

"The letters," Robert said. "Eighteen of them none shorter than 5 pages, started in the Spring of the year before she was killed. Philosophical stuff, issues of the day, no sex

105

for a long time but something more than a couple of friends chatting. Some clearly in response to her letters or calls. All written out in long hand. Insights into the lady. Reactions to how unhappy she was with her husband." Davison looked anywhere but at Will. "Toward the end, he wrote of a time they'd be together, the pain that it would cause their families, the joy they would have." Pause.

"Pretty romantic stuff all in all."

Will sat for what seemed like the longest time, the rest of his fried eggs gone cold. Walls down for no good reason other than he trusted the man across the table.

"When we were at the lake house right before he disappeared, Sam talked about whether Sharon was having an affair. I told you that before. They'd argued about it, but I don't think he really thought it was going on and neither did I."

"Will, I don't know what, if anything, this means. Neither does Olstrom, neither does my boss. But it's something that doesn't fit. I thought about rousting Silver myself and then had this brain storm that maybe you could call him cold and set up a meet. Olstrom thinks it wasn't a brain storm but more like a stroke and so does my boss. They think it's related to the stress of the divorce. Maybe so." Another pause, Davison deep in his head. Then, "But I still think it makes sense to have you do it. You know, in town for a conference or a deposition or whatever you people do, can't get the Greenbergs out of your head, you remembered the times you'd met, etc. etc. Then you do lunch, breakfast, something public so he won't shoot you. And a wire just in case he does, we'll get your last words. We'll be able to tell the judge how brave you were … or not."

It was Bennett's turn to laugh. Guy's a real comedian, he thought to himself. "Who does my estate get to sue if it goes bad?"

Davison. "Well, there is a small matter of the release our suits insist on before you do anything."

Joking again? Will pressed on. "So he agrees to meet with me for old times' sake. We get together, I spring the letters and say 'why'd you kill her?' Like that? And then he doesn't confess right away because he's a corporate lawyer and they don't do anything without billing 4 or 5 hours but he says 'Where did you get those?' And I say…what?"

"'Rachel gave them to me. Found them in a safe deposit box and didn't know who else to trust.'" Davison had thought that one through.

"Rachel hates my guts. How do we know she hasn't already told him?"

"She says she found them and brought them straight on to us. She promised no contact with Silver and says she's had none since the funeral. We have to trust her."

"Robert, why does he first of all meet with me at all? Everybody here thinks I know what happened. And even if he does meet with me and I say I know about the letters, why doesn't he just tell me to fuck off, get up and leave?"

"Because he's a corporate lawyer who doesn't do anything without billing 4 or 5 hours?" Davison's voice higher at the end for the question mark.

Bennett thought about it for a minute. He knew he would do it even before he left Albuquerque. He would've said 'no' over the phone and saved the trip if he had a brain in his head or had listened to his wife. But goddamn it, if Sam Greenberg were still alive and Will found him, he'd kill him himself and Sy Silver just might be part of the puzzle.

"OK. Let me read the letters, think about it, and maybe we can talk one more time before I call him."

"Sure Will, but the sooner the better."

"Robert, it's been eight months. This hasn't exactly been an express train."

Another pause. "Fair enough. There is the other thing we've got to talk about."

"OK. What?"

"The Russians."

CHAPTER TWENTY ONE
THE RUSSIANS

The Russians. Wilson Bennett felt a little dizzy and wondered for a second if it was the Gordon's talking back. The Russians.

"The Russians." Will looked around for some more coffee. "Who the hell are the Russians?"

Both of them refilled, Robert started in. "Rachel had mentioned off hand that her dad would sometimes gamble. She didn't know much about it other than what she heard around the dining room table. We worked Greenberg's friends, remembered what you had told us, and canvassed. Turns out the jeweler you talked about was on K, just down from Greenberg's office when he was in DC. Small time bookie, like you said, nothing big, but apparently worked with a bunch of folks including your friend and others.

"And?"

"About three years ago, Sam Greenberg got bored with the little stuff and wanted to go bigger. Our friend, the jeweler, knew some people who knew some people who knew some big time big timers being run by the Russian Mafia out of Brighton Beach. They'd been mostly in New York and on the West Coast but a few years ago, a small cell got started up in the DC area. Primarily gambling. Very very bad guys. It was the last time the guy ever saw Sam."

109

Will's mind was out of control. His good friend, the neurotic goofy silly very smart very good and very best friend was living a very double life that he had kept from his best friend for years. Wife with an affair, gambling with the Russians, wiping out life savings, buying guns. No wonder Sam had had a headache at the lake house.

He was seriously off plumb now. And feeling a little like Alice in Wonderland. The horror of eight months ago now back and worse than ever even as a normalcy had returned to life in New Mexico. This was an overload of information none of which made sense. If somebody had tried to put this in a book, nobody'd buy it. But here it was.

A deep breath Davison couldn't see. "Leads, thoughts?"

Davison's turn to take a breath. "We really have little to go on with the Russians. They are very deep, very small in numbers here, and not prone to undercover probes. We know they're here, Organized Crime tells us they're gaining influence with the gambling set, they make the American mob look like candy stripers, they are cold blooded killers by nature." Another breath.

"Any names of who Sam might have dealt with?"

"No."

"Addresses?"

"No."

"Paper trail?"

"None."

"Anything at all?"

"No. We don't even know for sure Greenberg was into the Russians except for the jeweler who has his own butt to cover. Do we think they killed Sharon Greenberg and grabbed her husband?" Davison paused. "Honestly, it doesn't add up. It would certainly not be above them to kill a loved one. Everybody knows that. But to disappear Greenberg makes no sense. Way I understand it, they'd kill the Mrs., kill Greenberg and put his head in bed with another deadbeat. This just doesn't fit."

"So what does?" If Bennett had any more coffee he'd float.

"Olstrom still likes Greenberg for the kill especially if he knew about Sy Silver." Will thinking he should have stuck to The Lie.

"There's motive, there's opportunity, it's Greenberg's gun, and he's nowhere to be found."

"You?"

"I had a friend once in college who was a neat freak. We were roommates for about a week, he came to me all apologetic but said he needed to be clean. So the college put him in a room by himself. Best year of my life but that's a whole other story. So I buy Sam and his OCD and Rachel confirms it. He'd never leave a mess even if he'd just killed his wife, especially if he'd just killed his wife. He was not dumb so why use his own gun? Why not use a baseball bat and wipe it clean? Why not make it look like a robbery? Why not make it look like the lover if he knew about him? So I just don't have the certainty I did eight months ago. And I want to run some rabbits down their holes."

"And here I am."

"And here you are."

"Are the Russians a dead end?"

"For now, for sure. No proof, no connection, no way to start looking. It's why we want to start with Sy Silver and see what he knows."

"And here I am."

CHAPTER TWENTY TWO
RACHEL

"How much of all of this does Rachel know?"

"All of it. She's the one who found the letters of course and brought them to us."

"What did she say about them?"

Thoughtful, Davison took a second. "Everybody does it differently, reacting to awfulness whatever it is. We've kept her up to date on what we've been doing and she's been pretty passive through it all. Tell you the truth, I would have expected even more anger, her mom's death, her thinking her dad did it. She still gets upset on the phone, still cries a lot but I think she's moving on.

Then she brings the letters in. She was home seeing about getting things in order and got to the safe deposit box and the letters. The box was only in her mother's name, she found the key in her mom's desk, and tracked it down. And when I asked her about her reaction, she said only 'I guess I'm not surprised.' Even though she never thought her mother was the one having an affair."

"Any hint she thinks Silver killed her?"

"To the contrary. She read all the letters and her reaction? 'At least somebody loved her.' She told me Sy Silver would never hurt a fly. That her dad must have found out and that's why he killed her. Rachel Greenberg is absolutely convinced her father is alive and well and living off what he took from the accounts."

Davison talking more than he knew he should but not wanting to stop.

"What's she make of the gambling? And the Russians?"

"Professes not to know anything. 'All I know is he murdered my mother.' Period, end of story."

"Is she OK?"

"I think so. Very guarded but who wouldn't be. Back in college and doing very well and getting enough aid to get her through. The nest egg is gone but she seems to be coming to grips even with that. But you mention her dad and make certain you're wearing Kevlar. She hates him with the only passion I see in her. For his sake, he's better off dead if she catches up with him"

Bennett recalled his own feelings about Sam and felt just a tad of kinship with his daughter.

"If you think of it and it seems appropriate, give her my love, would you?"

"Of course."

"So now what do we do?"

CHAPTER TWENTY THREE
READING SADNESS

More coffee than either of them needed but neither willing to switch to decaf before the other. Men, Bennett thought. More testosterone than brains. Wonder why this guy never has to pee?

Davison. This guy's amazing. Eight gallons of coffee and he doesn't have to pee. I'm dying here. Shit, I'm the guy with the badge. I can do whatever I want. "Give me a minute to get rid of some of this coffee, will you?" "Sure. Think I'll join you."

Two old lions struggling from the booth both in extremis. Small talk on the way to the men's room and then an embarrassingly long time at the urinals each trying to finish first and finally letting pride go in the interests of comfort. In the last analysis, who cared who won?

Back to the booth, both feeling the need to go again soon. Once the dam bursts.

"Robert, how are we going to do this?"

"This is what I think. Take the letters, go back to the room and read them. See what you think." Davison looked at his watch. 10:30. "Give me a call about 2. We'll have you come down, talk about the best approach. I'll get Olstrom and the chief too. Everybody agrees, we'll tap the phone and have you call. Late Thursday, you can give him the options of after work today, tomorrow at breakfast, tomorrow at lunch, tomorrow for a drink. Hard to say "no" to all of those."

Will nodded. Always good to have a plan that puts off the hard work.

They got up to leave, Davison insisting the bill was on the City of Alexandria, Will took the letters, and they shook hands on their way to their cars.

"Will, this is probably really half baked. But I'm glad you're here."

"Wouldn't have missed it for the world, Robert. I need this put to bed even worse than you."

They shook hands again and parted. Bennett waited for Davison to leave, got out of his car, and headed back into the diner knowing he'd never make the two blocks back to the hotel. On his way out of the john, he ran into Davison who'd driven around the block because he knew he'd never make it all the way to the station. And kicked himself for not seeing Bennett's rental still in the lot. They looked at each other and, for the first time in eight months for either of them, started to belly laugh at the absurdity of it all.

Except Davison was on the way in and couldn't dawdle.

Bennett laughed again to himself. Russian Mafia, homicide cops married to gay women, dead wives, bald lovers. Just my luck to buy this book in the airport.

He headed back to the Holiday Inn, pretty sure he'd make it and oblivious to the fact that this journey, in a few hours, would only get worse.

Back in the room, decaf now, and a call to Albuquerque. Alex was in her chambers in the middle of a criminal drug trial but anxious to hear from him. He gave her the Cliff's Notes version leaving out the irrelevant portions of the meeting but bringing her up to speed on Sy Silver, Rachel, the Russian Mob. It was a longer silence than he thought necessary. And then this.

"Be careful cowboy. I love you more than the moon and the sun. This is not altogether good stuff you're into. Be careful."

"I love you Alex. I wish you were here."

"Me too. Get 'er done and get home. Last time you leave without me. Last time."

"Bye." The click was like losing a link to sanity.

Wilson Bennett picked up the letters and began to read beginning to end.

They were all addressed to a PO Box in the Alexandria Post Office and Bennett was sure that it had been set up just for this purpose. He would check with Davison but would bet money there was another PO Box in the DC Metropolitan area in the name of Sy Silver.

At the beginning, they were relatively benign, talking of their kids, their lives, lost and forgotten dreams, health of parents, the kinds of things middle aged people talk about. Written with a fountain pen. Of course. He was a corporate lawyer, Will thought. That's all they ever use. Then in the fourth letter, Silver's tone changed. He spoke of a conversation he'd had with Sharon Greenberg about the desolation of his marriage and how much he hated going home and the emptiness of it all. Bennett remembered Silver's wife, thought them a perfect couple, and now knew how wrong he was. Silver spoke of the lack of intimacy and connection and this one ended, "And so, dear Sharon, I know exactly what you're feeling and thinking. Would there ever be a day...? Love, Sy."

Will stopped for a minute. November almost a year before she died. He tried to remember back to what was going on in Sam's parallel life but it was lost in the fog. Work problems? Health problems? Life problems? All of the above? Probably. But whatever, clearly a year before her death, Sharon Greenberg was a very unhappy woman.

The next letter not until January and obviously the relationship had changed. Sex most likely and the visual of Sy Silver naked was unsettling. "My dearest darling," it started and went downhill from there. The time together was like no other and, if he died tomorrow, it would be the memory of his life, blah, blah, blah. If Davison didn't think this was about sex, Will perversely thought he'd like to see some of the good stuff.

Reading the letters was like listening to one side of a telephone conversation and it was maddening. Because it was what was in Sharon's mind that was what Will needed to know. But there were glimpses of even another layer of his friend that he didn't know about. "For three days, you didn't know where he was?" "Sharon dear, why would he buy a gun? Are you scared?" Little incriminating things like that. Not that it was big time mind you. Sam Greenberg a man missing from everybody for three days buying a gun that would later kill his wife.

And a letter in the spring. Rachel had gotten pregnant and Silver's response was harsh. "I can't believe after all you have done for that slut, she would betray you like this. Just like kids. You give and give and they take and take and break your heart in the process. The anger in me says make her pack her bags and send her on her way. But I know you love her and must help her even with this horrible betrayal. I am so sorry. First your husband and now your precious daughter. What you must be thinking. But know this. I love you more than you can imagine. I'll never leave you. You are not alone. Forever, S."

He read them through the noon hour. Word for word. And his emotion was one of great sadness for two lost souls who, midst the chaos of life, had found an oasis of caring for each other.

Bennett had never thought that Sam and Sharon were a match but he thought they had made it work mostly around Rachel and all that she was accomplishing in her wonderful young life. Will had worried from time to time about what would happen when Rachel moved out but figured they would stay together more out of inertia than anything else.

And now it was clear that Sharon Greenberg needed out in the worst way. She'd fallen in love with a corporate lawyer.

The last letter was written in late October, days before she died. He had told his wife he wanted a divorce, that the marriage was empty and not worth saving or even working on. His wife had been calm almost to the point of coldness (Bennett thought aimlessly that maybe Sam was doing Mrs. Silver but that visual was even worse than Mr. Silver and Mrs. Greenberg and he drove it from his mind), said she understood, had already seen a lawyer, and was ready to move on with her life.

At first, heartbroken because of his wife's lack of emotional reaction, the letter continued on into one of happiness for a future for the two of them, where they would live (a place new to both of them), how they would tell their families (it would be very very hard), and the joy of a life together now they were rid of their demons. The kids were grown so they'd understand. "Tell him soon, my darling, so that we can start our new life together."

Sam had been at the lake house the day Sy Silver had written the last letter in the packet.

Will put the letters down, closed his eyes for a moment and thought, What Sam Greenberg did I know? The real one or this disconnected compulsive gambler, murderer. He ordered himself to go to a "Third Place" away from the sadness of the moment where his mind could simply be. Today the Third Place was the desert, a hot tub, some gin, and skin to skin with Alexandra Kennedy. Will Bennett wanted and needed home. And he lingered in the Third Place for a few precious minutes.

But there were some things that needed doing.

CHAPTER TWENTY FOUR
SETTING THE STING

At promptly 2:00 p.m., Will Bennett walked into the City of Alexandria Police Department on Mill Street and went directly to Homicide. Davison saw him walk in, waved him over to his cubicle, stood up and, file in hand, headed for a conference room. Lonnie Olstrom was already there and Will's first impression was way too many donuts over the past months and a need, far sooner than later, for some hair transplant appointments. Olstrom was subdued, shook Bennett's hand with only a nod of his head, and turned away. To Will's surprise, the Captain was an attractive 40something African American woman. She introduced herself simply as Alicia Young.

The four of them sat down and Davison began to lay out his plan. Bennett would go back to his hotel to avoid caller ID, and call Silver at his office. He would use the main switchboard to avoid suspicion. The police were sure Silver was in this afternoon (Will reminded himself that corporate lawyers rarely needed to leave their office) because he had been tailed by Alexandria's finest for two days expecting Bennett's arrival (so much for Bennett playing hard to get).

As Davison had previewed it at breakfast, Will is in town for the conference, still struggles with all that went on almost a year ago, and wonders if Sy would have a drink/lunch/breakfast/dinner with him just to catch up. Bennett can stay a day or two later if Silver's schedule is jammed today or tomorrow. Silver says "yes", they plan to meet. Silver says "no", Will says: 'Sy, Rachel gave me the letters you wrote her mother. We need to meet now.' Depending on the reaction, 'or I really need to get these to the police.' Geez, one of those truly ought to work.

Or, with a little bit of luck, Silver had had a heart attack earlier today and Will could get back to the desert where he belonged. A thought he would come back to in the days to follow.

Captain Young broke in. "Mr. Bennett, you're here because Detective Sergeant Davison thinks this will work. You're a private citizen and have no obligation whatsoever to do this. None whatsoever." Will saw her look at Davison. "If you do, we're grateful, but if anything happens, you're on your own." This would be the signing of the release the lawyers had written.

"I'm in. I'm guessing there's something you want me to sign?"

Young and Bennett looked each other over for a long moment. Will saw in her some of the same steel his wife had, some of the same sense of purpose, and something else, a sadness around the small lines at the corners of her eyes.

Without question in Will's mind, Alicia Young had earned her bars the hard way.

The captain broke the gaze and looked at Olstrom who pulled a multi page document from his notebook and slid it over to Bennett who gave it a cursory review, went to the last page, and signed. "Harvest my organs, will you, Robert?" Over Olstrom's head but Young couldn't suppress a smile. Ever the professional, Sergeant Detective said quietly, "Of course, Mr. Bennett."

Davison went back to business. "I'll go with you to the hotel along with our techie to get the phone set for tapping. If he agrees to meet with you today, she'll also set you up with a wire and how to use it. OK?"

A little too much either adrenaline or caffeine from this morning but Will couldn't resist. He looked at Olstrom. "Lonnie?" He knew he'd hate that. "What do you think?"

Detective Olstrom's face took on a very unhealthy purple pallor. His mouth opened once or twice to say something and Will was struck by how very much he looked like a fish. What's Alex's line? About as wide between the eyes as a perch? Perfect. Olstrom nodded his head to give only the most minimal approval to what clearly was close to making him stroke out. He may even have made a sound but nothing human enough to understand.

They all stood. Captain Young shook his hand and wished him well. Olstrom did neither. And Davison and Bennett were alone.

"Well, that went well, don't you think?" Davison asked Will.

And the only thing Bennett could think of was the last time he'd said that to himself, there'd been hell to pay.

CHAPTER TWENTY FIVE
THE CALL

The "techie" was a just out of college/computer school young woman who loved both piercings and tattoos. Clearly more comfortable with computers than people.

Breaking the ice back at the hotel, Will asked her: "So Jackie, how did you get involved with police work?" A soft ball.

"Only job I could get."

"What do you like about it?"

"Good benefits." Bennett saw Davison smile. "Anything else?"

Jackie stopped her work for a minute coming to the realization that she would have to communicate with a human. She looked at him for a moment.

"Not really." And went right back to work on the phone.

In a few minutes, Jackie stood up, gathered her tools, and declared the job done. "Soon as he picks up the phone and dials '7' for a local, it kicks in." She took a second. "Good luck, Pops."

"Thanks Jackie." Will was just about to stick out his hand to say good bye but she was out the door clearly in a hurry to get back to the van parked outside the hotel to wait and see whether they needed her again. Davison and Bennett looked at each other and both knew what the other was thinking. Kids, whadda you gonna do?

It was 3:30. Even Will assumed the corporate types were back from lunch by then. He took a deep breath, looked at Robert who nodded, and dialed the number. A very sterile voice answered, he asked for Sy Silver, was put on hold, and a very pleasant, very English, very warm voice announced he had gotten so far as Mr. Silver's gate keeper.

"Is Mr. Silver available?"

"Who may I say is calling?"

"Wilson Bennett from Michigan and New Mexico. I'm a friend of the Goldbergs. Mr. Silver and I have met several times."

A pause. "I'll see if he's available."

A longer pause. The very pleasant voice back. "I'm sorry, Mr. Silver is quite tied up at the moment. Can he call you back?"

"I'd very much like to talk with him today. I'm in town for a conference and it would be great to see him again."

Another long pause. "I'm sorry, he is so busy."

Pissed now as he always got dealing with big city lawyers. "Tell Mr. Silver I've read his letters to Ms. Sharon Greenberg of the Greenberg Foundation, am very impressed with the scholarly, legalistic approach he has taken and would like to speak with him about them. Today. Now." A glance at Davison in the corner nodding approval.

A much shorter pause.

"Sy Silver," a voice Will recognized from the Bat Mitzvah lunch.

"Sy, thanks for taking my call," Yeah, right. "Will Bennett here wondering if we could get together tonight for a drink? Lot to talk over, don't you think?"

Back to a longer pause. Will wondered what corporate giant was paying for this call. "Mr. Bennett, I'm sorry, you've caught me at a very bad time. Perhaps the next time you're in town?"

"Sy," (may I call you Sy, Will thought to himself), "Sy, Rachel gave me the letters you wrote Sharon Greenberg over the last eighteen months before she died. I've read them, Rachel has read them, and so far, nobody else. That can change. You were having an affair with her and that is something the Alexandria police and/or the bar association would be very interested in." (The bar association piece was ridiculous; if the local bar association of any state had to investigate stuff like this, nothing would ever get done. Like Congress).

Davison listened with an increasing respect for the hard edge Will Bennett had just added to the mix. Cops and his bar ticket all in one sentence.

Bennett heard the audible breath across the phone line. "I could meet you for a few minutes tonight after work." Silver's voice almost a whisper.

Hale fellow well met again, Will said, "Name the time and place and I'll be there." Silver named the time and a downtown hotel. Bennett, who knew the place from the one time Sam had taken him there, hoped either Silver or the police were buying even if it was just for drinks. "I'll be there." He hung up and looked at Davison who went to get Jackie to set the wire.

CHAPTER TWENTY SIX
ON THE RECORD OFF THE RECORD

The Hay Adams Hotel represents all that is venerable and historic and political and rich that is the fabric of Washington, D.C. Which of course is why Sy Silver picked it and why Will Bennett hated it. Clearly, Silver wanted Will to know that this was his town. But Will had the letters.

Built as a beautiful lady in the 1920s in Lafayette Square at the corner of Sixteenth and H Streets, she had been hostess to many of the world's most important people. Silver had picked the Off the Record bar as the meeting place. Will had called Alex and they had both giggled over the concept of being someplace called Off the Record wired to the police van parked across the street. That would be irony.

But after they had hung up, she had paused and whispered to the goddess to keep her love safe. This was uncharted territory especially for somebody like Will.

Will Bennett walked into the Hay Adams and into the Off the Record as though he owned it. His off the rack suit fit pretty well and, with a little help from his wife, he could still put the right shirt with the right tie with the right shoes and socks at least six times out of ten. Better than that when she helped him pack. He carried the small microphone that Jackie had put in his pocket.

He saw Silver across the way in a booth in the corner and walked over.

"Sy, how are you? Been a long time." Midwest warm and fuzzy.

Silver looked back at him not buying it for a heartbeat. He had put on a lot of weight, wore a dark pinstripe suit that cost a boat load more than Will's but was at least a size or two too small. He looked very tired with deep dark circles under his eyes and a waxy pallor to his skin. But still handsome in a balding corporate sort of way. Aging zaftig was a description that came to mind.

"Will."

An obligatory brief weak, wet hand shake.

Will slid into the booth, took more time than necessary to get comfortable, and then looked into Silver's eyes. Silver stared back, then broke the gaze, and Bennett knew the man to be very scared. "Sy, what do you hear from Rachel, anything?"

Blessedly for Sy, the waitress came up. Silver ordered a double Bombay Sapphire up, Will a Jameson's on the rocks.

Finally, Silver answered. "Nothing since the funeral. You know that or you wouldn't be here. You said you found some letters. What do you want?"

So much for chit chat. Will let the 'how's the little woman and the kids' question go.

"For about 18 months before her death, the two of you wrote each other using post office boxes as a cover (educated guess on the part of Davison and Bennett that, if there was one, there were two) for a relationship that may have started out innocently but, by the time she was killed, was a full blown sexual affair."

The drinks and some peanuts came. Most expensive drinks in the world and they serve peanuts? Will longed for the Coppertop in Albuquerque or the local tavern in Michigan. He could do places like this but hated them. He wondered idly if his zipper were up, thought about checking, and then got concerned the techies in the van would hear it. He'd check later.

"Sharon Greenberg was the love of my life," Silver started almost as if it were a relief to get it out in the open. "I loved her for thirty years ever since I met her in undergrad. She never knew it but I followed her around like a puppy the two years we were at UMass, lost track of her after graduation, and then we met again in DC by chance. I was out of law school and just starting as an associate with the firm, she had moved here after undergrad and was working on the Hill for a Senator."

He caught his breath, took a drink, and went on. "I was having a drink with a friend after work and saw her across the way with a tall guy. It was this very bar and Sam was her date."

Will looked at him and it was almost as though he had transported himself back, what, twenty five years ago?

"I screwed up every ounce of courage this body could muster and went over and said hello. I don't think she even remembered who I was. But she was so kind and so good, she asked me and my friend to join them. Had I one ounce of self respect, I would have said no and never looked back but I sat down and we joined them."

Bennett was pretty sure Jackie in the van had either dozed off or left for some caffeine and sugar, certain she was not going to miss anything important at least for half an hour. He wished he could do the same.

"That night, I got the sense of just how big an asshole Sam Greenberg was. Pompous, arrogant, fancied himself a real ladies' man, monogrammed shirt," Will noted Silver's monogram on his shirt cuff, SDS. That would be irony. "But at the end of the night, I had struck up a relationship with Sam, knowing it was the only way to get connected again to Sharon. And the friendship began."

"You were married?" "Oh yeah, married Barbara in law school and our first child was born my third year." "Still married?" A pause longer than it should be. "After a fashion."

133

This was easier than Will ever imagined it would be. It was clearly cathartic for Silver. "Then what?"

"For the next 25 years, I yearned and fantasized. We'd see them from time to time socially and sometimes I'd plan activities that I knew she would be at. Day she got married, I drank a whole bottle of vodka and was sick for three days. But it didn't matter. I got Barbara to buy a house closer to where Sam and Sharon had bought in Virginia just to be close."

This was so pathetic Will thought about telling him he was wired and calling it a night.

"Was it a good marriage for the two of them?"

"At the start, I don't know. We didn't see them all that much. We had our first child, then Rachel was born, and then our second. I'd still do the drivebys and the chance meetings or sometimes at Temple but I was busy at work trying to make partner and trying to put her out of my mind. We moved in roughly the same set and I'd see them at large parties.

And then that all changed about eighteen months before she died."

Sy Silver stopped and he began to cry. Not a tear up but a major sob thing. Will thought about asking for more peanuts. Jesus. He hoped Jackie was picking up the sobs.

Finally, Silver took his napkin, blew his nose, wiped his eyes and, in a very small voice, said, "Sorry."

Will shook his head. "Nothing to be sorry for, Sy. I feel bad we're doing this." Hear that, Davison?

"We all had been at a pool party at some friends' house in August, the usual crowd, but I saw Sharon across the room and she'd clearly been crying. I got her alone in the den and asked about her. And all she said was, 'I never thought I could be so lonely.' And she left. A few days went by and I called her for lunch. And she said yes."

The plot thickens. Will felt dirty especially because he knew that Jackie was in the van thinking 'Yuk, old people.' He wondered what Jackie did when she wasn't sitting in a cramped van with a couple of other techies and Davison with headphones on listening to one more little dirty secret. What a depressing view of life. Attention back to Sy Silver.

"We met up in Maryland at a little place on Wisconsin Ave. She was as beautiful as ever and very sad. For the next three hours, she told me about the sham she lived every day of her life with Sam. It was after that we decided to write each other. Friends. That's all."

"At some point that changed."

"We got closer and closer through letters and calls. She told me the whole story about life with Sam and it was crazy making."

Will was pretty sure he wasn't going to like what was coming. Preserved for posterity on a machine in a police van across the way.

"Sam Greenberg is an asshole. Always was. Never changed." Will noted the present tense. "He took the best woman in the world and made her life a living hell." Raw anger and pure rage. Jesus, the techies better be getting this.

"He abused his wife, abused his daughter, had I don't know how many affairs, gambled, drank, gone for weeks on end. Awful. Awful shit." Quieter sobs, another nose blow.

Will reminded himself he was on the wire. Patience. Keep him talking.

"What do you mean 'abuse'"?

"He never hit them, I guess, but did everything else he could to make their lives a living hell. Every night, he'd yell at her or Rachel for anything he could find fault with, cooking, cleaning, school work, wash. Every single day and night was a horror."

Silver stopped, drank, and ordered another.

"How long?" Bennett asked.

"From the very beginning."

"And Rachel?"

"Rachel grew up with a shell of hardness that even her father couldn't get through. As soon as she could, she got involved in every extracurricular activity she could just so she didn't have to be home any more than she had to. She was good at everything she touched. Trouble was, that included drugs and drinking. She began to run with a bad crowd and not even Sam screaming at her or grounding her made her change. It only got worse. Senior in high school, she got pregnant. Sharon set up the appointment with the clinic and it was over just before the holidays. Sam never knew."

"Sharon was a very smart, very strong woman. Why didn't she leave? Why didn't she call the police? Why not get divorced?"

"Because your best friend was a prick. Sharon had a past, petty criminal record, some drugs, nothing huge but Sam held it over her, threatened to get custody of Rachel, and leave her penniless. And she bought it."

"Why not come to you? You're a lawyer, you could have helped."

"Shame I guess. We were at a New Year's party at the Greenbergs the year he killed her. She came up to me, slipped me a note saying she wanted to see me as soon as she could. We met for a drink two days later, went to a hotel and never looked back"

"What changed on New Year's?"

"When Sharon found out Rachel was pregnant and had to set up the abortion, she told me she really began to unravel. There was nobody. Right before everybody got there, Sam and she had a huge blowout about something, he was calling her names and, with everything else, she snapped."

"So why the letter so critical of Rachel down the way? If you knew the horror of the truth? Why?"

"Because Sharon blamed herself, thought it was all her fault for not having the courage to leave the son of a bitch. That if she had, Rachel's life would have been so different. I was trying to say the right things to help get her through it."

Even Will Bennett had his limits. Tired of this man, tired of the story, tired of what he knew to be lies, tired of a pathetic, self flagellating man trying to be a hero in his own mind.

"Speaking of the right things, Sy, did you think it was the right thing to be fucking around on your wife and kids?" A tad hypocritical, Will, just a tad.

Silence and a sudden chill. Silver was now not quite so confessional. He ordered another drink. Bennett hung on to the Jameson's. And the peanuts.

"Why should I tell you a fucking thing other than what an asshole your best friend is?"

"'Is? Why the present tense, Sy?"

"Is, was, will be. Mother fucker should never have been allowed to crawl out from under a rock. What does it matter?"

Will was thinking that none of this was ringing quite true but put it on the shelf to mull over later. Back to the present. "Here's the answer to your question, Sy. Because I have the letters, because I know whether you're lying or not, because the letters will probably have to go to the police and because you'll have to tell them about the affair. Or get charged with Sharon Greenberg's murder."

Pause. And then the closer.

"Here's why it matters. Thirty years of longing for her and finally, two days after New Years, fantasy is reality, you're screwing the princess." Harsher than he wanted probably but he needed a strong finish.

Silver took a long drink and said nothing.

"Did you kill her, Sy? Did you kill her because she wouldn't leave the 'monster'"?

A whisper. "No. I loved her. Always did, always will." Back to sobbing. "We were going to be together. That was the deal. She would tell Sam with Rachel off to college, I'd tell Barbara and the kids and it would happen. I would never kill her."

"Where were you the day she was killed?"

"Hawaii. Second honeymoon. Telling Barbara I wanted a divorce."

Now that's a second honeymoon.

139

Timing. The waitress appeared and Will ordered another Jameson's, Sy a third double Bombay.

CHAPTER TWENTY SEVEN
REQUIEM

Both men paused to get a breath, both exhausted by the conversation.

Will was quieter. "I guess it's none of my business, Sy, nope, I know it's none of my business but would you tell me about those months before Sharon was killed?" Silver was still trying to compose himself.

"The best, the worst, all the in between. Greenberg always traveling or always doing something so we had a lot of time together. Rachel was doing everything under the sun and rarely home. Her mom was trying to deal with the pregnancy and demanding that Rachel get an abortion. Barbara thinking as long as the money's coming in, who cares? Kids clueless. I was never around on a good day. Why worry now? The best, the worst."

Will had to know. "Their house, their bed?"

Silver knew why he asked, debated lying, but it was past that. "Yes."

Game face again. "What was the plan?"

"We'd lived lies for almost 18 months. Me for years. The plan was to tell our spouses, take the hits, hope that our kids would forgive us, and live a life of truth. And love."

"When was the last time you saw her?"

A very long pause. "Two nights before she died, we had dinner together. I was leaving first thing the next morning for Hawaii. We talked of where we were, where we'd been, where we could be. She would tell him while I was gone. We had a 7 a.m. flight out of Dulles. Three days later, my assistant called to tell me Sharon was dead."

"If you didn't kill her, who did?" Had to ask and knew the answer.

Face flushed, sweating, Silver took a deep breath. "Greenberg killed her, you know it, I know it, everybody knows it. She told him the nightmare was over and he killed her. End of story. And he runs. And runs. And runs forever." Silver was rubbing his shoulder through his suit coat.

"Still alive?"

"Sure. Of course. Why not? Wipes out the accounts. Living in Belize. Mexico. Costa Rica. Someplace."

But Sy Silver had not seen Rachel Greenberg since the funeral. So he'd know about the accounts how? He was still rubbing his shoulder, still sweating, still flushed.

Silver stood up, threw down some bills, and announced he was leaving. He stepped from the booth with a nod of his head to Will and headed out.

And collapsed like a helium balloon out of gas. Eyes rolling up, Bennett at his side, a crowd gathering, seconds passing, Will loses the carotid pulse and begins CPR with a stranger from a table or two over. Five to one, five to one, five to one. EMTs next to him, defibrillation paddles, mechanized CPR, on a gurney and out the door. For Will it took seconds or hours, he would never quite know which.

Back to real time, there was a cop asking for ID, Will was giving an edited version of the conversation, local address, and being told to call the police at the Lafayette Square station to set up an appointment to give a full statement in the morning.

Almost sleep walking, Will walked out of the hotel, got a cab, and went to the hospital. In the ER, Bennett was told Silver had been taken back to a room and they'd be out to talk to him. He settled into a plastic something they called a chair and waited. Minutes later, maybe thirty, maybe longer, a gaunt, well dressed, very pinched woman walked in with a woman who had to be her sister. Will heard her announce that she was Barbara Silver and was told to take a seat. For whatever reason, Will thought about reintroducing himself, but knew that even if she looked at him, she'd have no clue who he was. And he chose to give the impression he was there for somebody else.

Not long after, a nurse came out of the back and asked for Mrs. Silver. She rose and, with her friend or sister, went through the doors.

143

Bennett waited, saw Barbara Silver and her sister come out 20 minutes later, composed, and alone. He knew Sy Silver was dead.

He stood, stretched, and headed for the door and the fresh air of the Washington night. Davison was there on the sidewalk. "Ride?"

Bennett nodded yes, Davison found Bennett's upper arm with his hand, and guided him to an unmarked marked van parked behind Davison's unmarked marked car. As they approached, Jackie got out of the van, quietly reached into Will's suit coat pocket and pulled the microphone out. She looked at him with a strange mixture of sympathy and kindness and something else. A touch of the macabre?

"That happen to you a lot, Pops?" She squeezed his arm, turned, and got back in the van.

Quirky, Will thought to himself, as he got into Davison's car and relaxed for the first time in a very long time.

CHAPTER TWENTY EIGHT
DECOMPRESSION

They rode in silence, Davison driving, Bennett looking out the window at the tall buildings, lights on, loneliness, sadness. Heading back across the 14th Street Bridge to Virginia.

"Dinner?" Davison.

"Yes."

Davison drove to a road house off the beaten path, certainly known only to the locals, a few pickups in the lot, not a single license plate other than the great state of Virginia. Perfect. A booth and beers ordered.

They sat in silence for a long time. Beers arrived, peanuts in the shell to throw on the floor, and burgers ordered.

Finally. "You listened to it all?"

"Yes."

"And?"

"And?' to you. You were there with him. Go first."

Will took a breath. He'd been with both his dad and mom when they'd died and with a close friend the last night of his life. But this was different. Conversation. Confession. Collapse. A man who he knew almost nothing about but who was so central to this drama. And now dead. And the worst part? Bennett was numb. No real feeling at all. Not connected to the body now in the morgue waiting to be cut to pieces in the morning, hours now from the Off the Record, hours from his lips on the man's mouth still tasting of Bombay, less than hours from the ER and seeing Silver's wife in the waiting room. He wondered again if the other woman was a sister and hoped it was. He knew he should feel more but he simply didn't.

And so he returned to the conversation.

"He believed what his filter told him to believe. I have known Sam Greenberg for thirty plus years, seen him with Sharon, watched the love he had for Rachel, talked about his life at least once a week. For whatever reason, Silver's filter is way out of sync with my take."

"Any sense any of it could be true?"

"It is so far off what I know to be a different couple, different lives, different everything."

"Why then?"

Bennett shook his head, drank some beer, ate some peanuts, and said nothing. And finally shook his head again. He raised his head and looked at his friend.

"I have not a fucking clue, Robert."

The burgers mercifully arrived and both men dug into them. Will, true to years of vegetarianism to pacify his daughter, with his tuna burger and Robert with a half-pound thing dripping with grease and cheese that was damn near scary. Fries, two more beers and there was almost a sense of normalcy.

Except Sam Greenberg was still missing, his wife was still dead, his wife's lover was dead, and eight months later, there were still more questions than answers.

Alex. I need to get home.

CHAPTER TWENTY NINE
CALL   HOME   WILL

Robert dropped an exhausted Will off at the Holiday Inn with the plan they would meet in the morning at the station, talk over where they were, and get Will on a plane back to the desert Friday afternoon in time to have a weekend.

He called Alex as soon as he was alone in his room. She was home watching movies and snuggled in bed. He brought her up to date on what had happened leaving nothing out. At the end of the story, he paused to get his breath.

Finally Alex. "Wow. How are you?"

"Numb, absolutely numb. I was there, I listened to the whole story. I got sad, I got mad, I got defensive, I got all kinds of emotions. Then the guy falls over dead, I do CPR on him, I go to the ER, turns out he's deader than dead, and I feel nothing. Really."

"Why do you think?"

"God, I don't know. You'd think I'd be just a little upset watching this guy die before my eyes. It's like this whole eight months has been somebody else's life being shown through my body. It's just surreal, just weird. Here he is, a major player in Sam's life, in Sharon's life, and now he's gone."

"Heart?"

"Must have been. Unless it was the peanuts. But then I'd be dead. And I'm not."

"You sure?"

"Pretty sure. I'll get back to you when I know for certain." He could almost see her smile across the miles.

"Just save that one thing, OK? And if you're dead, see if you can donate that one thing to me."

Bennett laughed, a relief after a very long day. "Tell me something normal."

"Tom and Melinda want to go to an Isotopes game with us Saturday night."

"That would be very good."

"Davison is going to continue to keep you connected to this case until it's over. That's for sure. And you're going to let him. And that's for sure. So far it reads like a dime store novel. Russian mafia, lovers, make that dead lovers, disappearing friends, dead or alive, dead wives. I know you want to be involved but you'll end up more of the problem than the solution. Davison just doesn't know that about you yet."

For Kennedy, it was a speech.

"OK." Pause. "You're right."

"What? Just like that?"

Tired beyond words. "Just like that."

"Get some sleep, will you? Call me when you know when you're getting in. And your flight's guaranteed. Oh, and I love you, big boy."

Bennett went to bed, weird dreams of lifeless bodies, guns, blood, police lights, sirens. At one point, he woke up in a sweat, got up, got some water, and wondered about the peanuts.

CHAPTER THIRTY
WHAT NEXT

The next morning at 9 a.m. he was back on Mill Street. Same journey to homicide, same conference room with Detective Sergeant Davison and Captain Young, only missing Olstrom. "Another assignment," was all Davison would give Bennett for the absence. Will didn't miss him much.

Young took control. "Sergeant Detective Davison still thinks your friend is innocent. Even after you conveniently kill a key witness." She allowed herself a smile. "I disagree and I'm sure Detective Olstrom will feel the same. Especially after he hears the wire." She paused. "But I'll give you that there are a couple of things that are troublesome. The Russians, the lover, the missing gun, the OCD stuff." She allowed herself a raised eyebrow. "And, most importantly, we don't have anybody to arrest because we can't find your friend. And we don't even know if he's dead or alive.

From all accounts, he's such a doofus he almost has to be dead because he isn't smart enough to be on the run, and we can't find him." Another pause. "I'm sorry, Mr. Bennett, that was uncalled for."

Will was doing Buddha and said nothing. Young went on.

"So. Where does this go from here? Lover dead, husband gone, money all gone. Husband does it, kills his wife in a rage with his own gun when she tells him about Silver while Silver is in Hawaii for his second 'honeymoon', tries to disappear with no identity and no money, has already wiped out the accounts, gets caught by the Russians, and is a goner. With Jimmy Hoffa someplace." She was harsh again and meaning to be. Because of what came next.

"So why not call it a day, leave it with the media that all the evidence points to Greenberg who has disappeared, shut down the investigation, send Mr. Bennett back to…" a pause and a look at her notes "…Albuquerque, and, if something happens, if something important and relevant happens, we put the band back together? Case over until further notice. Davison and Olstrom go on to something else."

Bennett didn't have to look at Davison to know that this was Bennett's turn, the detective deferring to his captain and leaving it to Will to state the case.

"Captain Young. If you shut it down and declare it over, then we never know the truth, and none of the Greenbergs, Sam, Sharon or Rachel, ever get justice. There's no suspect, no murder weapon, no provable motive, no proof of gambling, nothing to prove a case if you ever had to bring it to a prosecutor or grand jury. And Rachel lives forever thinking that her dad killed her mom. None of us know that. The Detective Sergeant and I don't believe it. It's like you're giving up."

Bennett had liked Young the first time he had met her. He respected her and understood why she was making the decision she was making. It was about job security, about politics, about being a black woman in a Virginia police department. It was about shutting down a costly investigation that had no end in sight. And a couple of loose ends, one of whom she knew and trusted and one of whom was a lawyer from some God forsaken land she'd only read about, who kept nibbling and noodling.

"Mr. Bennett. Seven years ago, my sister was murdered in Southeast DC. Car jacking. When they found the car two days later, she was dead in the passenger seat of gun wounds from an untraceable Saturday night special. She had been on her way to day care to pick up her two kids. They live with me now because there was nobody else to take care of them. They never found the mother fucker who killed her. And she was a cop's sister." She was quiet, under control.

"So I know what rage and anger and sadness and grief and wondering why is all about. I pray every day that some asshole is arrested on a traffic charge and connects up to who killed my sister so I can tell her kids there is justice in this world. But it hasn't happened yet. Maybe never.

Robert, off the record, you'll keep this investigation open. You'll do it on your own time, you'll not involve anybody other than me if you find anything out, and you'll continue to keep Mr. Bennett informed on a weekly basis."

"Yes, Ma'am." Davison stood. Captain Young looked at Will Bennett. "It's all about justice, Mr. Bennett. I hope we can find it for all of our sakes."

"Thank you, Captain."

"Thank you, Mr. Bennett."

Davison. "Let me take you to the airport, Will."

Will dared a glance at his watch. 10:15. Flight's at 2. This time of day from the police station to National, tops, 15 minutes. No bags to check. "That'd be great. That should get me there with even a little time to spare." Like two and a half hours.

Bennett stood and shook hands with Alicia Young. And then hugged her. For the bond only those that have had to live through unspeakable tragedy would understand.

Into the bright sunshine of a hot June Virginia morning.

"Sophie's for some breakfast and to kill some time?"

"Whatever." Will settled into the unmarked marked car.

Whatever.

An odd time on a work day and they practically had the diner to themselves. They were comfortable with each other especially after the last 24 hours.

"Will, I'll keep at it when I can but you have to know that turning anything up will be a miracle. Greenberg's trail, if there is one, is very cold, people are moving on with their lives, Rachel especially. We just may never know what happened to him. Or who for sure killed Sharon Greenberg."

Bennett looked into his coffee for a long time mulling over the words of surrender. He knew Davison was right, knew it in his head, just not his heart. He finally looked up.

"I know. Alex has told me that, you've told me that, and I've told me that. Maybe so. But it just is not Sam."

Gentleness in the Detective Sergeant. "Sometimes people lead lives that only they can figure out. Look at Rebecca. Married, two kids, stud for a husband. And gay. Imagine what she went through." A pause for effect. "Look what we know now that you never knew about your best friend. Big time gambling caught up with the Russians, Sharon with a lover, claims of emotional abuse through their whole married life. You knew none of that."

If any of it is true, Will thought to himself. "Maybe so, Robert, maybe I'm just being stubborn because I don't want to believe it. And maybe it's time to get back to the desert and get on with life."

Davison nodded. "I think so."

"What about you, my friend? What happens to you and the kids?"

155

Robert, thoughtful, eyes focused now on his coffee. "It's so trite but it really is a day at a time. It's awful and it ought to be. And I know it isn't easy on Rebecca either. She loves the kids and she knows the pain she's causing. For the next little while, it's about the kids and then maybe later, I'll get some color back in this life."

Davison paid again on the city and they drove to the airport.

"Robert, would you ever think about coming out to New Mexico for a visit? You could bring the kids, there's lots to do, or just come by yourself. We could show you some of the sights, introduce you to the Land of Enchantment. Think it over?"

"I sure will. Sounds very good." They shook hands, hugged briefly, and Will was into the terminal. Unmarked marked drove away.

CHAPTER THIRTY ONE
BACK HOME IN THE DESERT

Saturday morning they were still in bed and loving every minute of it. The peacefulness of morning love making that they never tired of but this time even more languid for there was nothing but the day ahead of them. They had talked until midnight with a bottle of Australian Shiraz around the patio and the hot tub. Alex had listened to the detail of the trip without interruption and when he got to Davison's advice to simply get on with life, she nodded her approval.

That is what he would do. Saturday morning was the first day of life with Sam Greenberg somewhere in a compartment of his brain every once in awhile to be taken out and examined but, as much as possible, to rest there while Will and Alex got on with the rest of their lives.

Grace, with a year off, was now ready to tackle law school, Will and Liz were busy taking on new cases and new challenges, and the Honorable Alexandra Kennedy was dispensing daily justice.

Alex and Will spent two weeks at the lake house seeing old friends and walking long walks on the beach and in the woods and bicycle trips on the beautiful West Michigan country roads. Life was almost returning to normal. Almost.

Robert was now down to calling every other week or sometimes just emailing. There was nothing new to report on the case, really, and it was more just a chance to keep a friendship alive. The divorce had gone through, Robert and Rebecca shared custody, and Davison seemed to be getting to a point where there would be life after the pain.

Over Labor Day, Will called and invited Robert and his kids out to Albuquerque for the Balloon Festival in October. It surprised both of them when Robert said yes. He made the arrangements, got the kids to take three days out of school, and they spent a magical long weekend at the festival seeing the thousands of balloons and all of the activity and working in side trips in the gondola to the top of the Sandias, the Natural History museum, Old Town, touristy stuff. The kids, polite almost to a fault, seemed to love every minute of their time and were great. Robert, Jr. even liked green chili, although Fran was much more cautious. Robert was content, talked of having had some dates, and was clearly moving on. Friends comfortable with each other, Alex seeing a side of Davison she had only known through Will's eyes. Genuinely coming to like him.

Sam Greenberg came up the second night the Davison family was there once the kids were off to bed and Alex, Will and Robert were having a glass of wine on the patio. "We got nothing, you guys. Not a whisper about anything. We ran Sy Silver's story and it all checked out. His wife said they'd had a great time in Hawaii and were more in love than ever. 'I'm still so devastated he's gone'. Post showed major blockage and massive m.i. If not that Thursday night, then very soon. He was a vertitable time bomb. The Greenbergs' house sold finally and the proceeds went to Rachel and that will help. She's a sophomore at UVA and apparently doing well. Not a whisper about Greenberg, never found the gun, tried to run the Russians for a bit and got nowhere. I think it's over."

Alex relieved, Will resigned. "Robert, you did everything you could. Thank you for believing."

Davison nodded. "One more thing. DC Metro does a traffic stop on some bangers in Anacostia, search the car on a pretext, and come up with a gun that matches ballistics with the gun that killed Captain Young's sister. Got a 22 year old small time drug dealer who 'fesses to the car jacking when he's 15. Plus a bunch of other stuff. Can't say it made much difference in Captain Young's attitude but maybe there is some justice after all."

The trio raised their glasses to Lady Justice.

Alex took a day off from the bench and shepherded the Davison family around the local hang outs. At least those that were PG. She and Robert talked of old loves, old history, avoided the Greenberg case by mutual silent consent, and, in the midst of the energy of his kids, came to know each other to a depth that surprised them both.

The next day Alex drove the Davison clan to the airport. Robert Jr. and Fran dominated the trip with talk of their New Mexico adventures and promises to come back as soon as their Dad would let them. She let them out at the American Airlines entrance and hugged Robert. Longer than it should have been. And less than they wanted? What was that about?

A tad breathless. "You've been a very good friend. To both of us. Thank you." Her eyes intent on his.

"Alex, I wish it were different. You know that."

A last hug, briefer. "Safe travels, Robert."

Back in the car, Alex looking in the mirror and noticing the flush in her cheeks. What was that about?

And that night, for the first time in all of the nights they had been together, Alex's mind strayed to another man. What truly the hell was that about?

JOURNEY'S END

CHAPTER THIRTY TWO
MESSAGE FROM NOWHERE

Mid November, more than a year after Sharon Greenberg's death, Liz LaRue got home after work, opened her mailbox, and found a postcard showing the beach of Lake Michigan just north of the pier five miles from the lake house. "Wish You Were Here" scrawled in rough printed marker. Postmarked three days before. Nothing else. She took it inside and looked at it for a long time. She called her daughter in Michigan who disavowed any knowledge of it and then she called Will.

Alex, Karen, Will and Liz met at Seasons for a drink, the post card in the middle of the table. Each of them would look at it, turn it over, inspect it, then put it back down for the next person. Silence for a long time.

Finally Karen. "It has to be him. Who else?"

"How does he know where I live?" Liz.

"When you moved out here, he called and was going to send some flowers and I gave him your address." Will. "Did he?" An afterthought.

"Nope."

Figures.

Alex. "So what does it mean? He's alive. He's in Michigan. He's at the lake house? He wants you to go there?

"

Why not call you directly? Why send an anonymous card to Liz? "

"Because he's alive and on the run from something or somebody and thinks contacting me directly would be dangerous," Will was thinking out loud. "So he sends it to the person he knows is a degree separated from you and me but still knowing enough to connect the dots. Not to the house, not to you Alex, and certainly not to me."

More silence. Karen said. "He wants you to go to Michigan, to the lake house. He's there or close by and he's on the run." The other three nodded. Unanimous.

Will looked at Liz who didn't miss a beat. "I'll have to check for sure but I think the next couple of weeks are pretty clear. New Mexico. Prepping for the holidays takes more time than the holidays themselves. Nothing that can't be covered."

Alex looked at Karen. "I'll have to check for sure but I think the next couple of weeks are pretty clear." Karen looked at Liz. "New Mexico. Prepping for the holidays…" Liz and Karen thought themselves hysterically funny.

"Let's think this through." Alex started. "He sends a post card snail mail to a connection that he knows well but with no guarantee that Liz puts it together. So he's some place that he thinks is safe at least for now. Let's say he's right to be paranoid and let's say for the sake of argument, the

163

something or somebody knows about us. And let's say after all this time, we're being watched." Liz quietly picked the card up and put it in her purse. "Hang with me. So you and I jump a plane to Michigan in mid November in a heart beat. If he's right and we're right, and that's a stretch, are we leading somebody to him? And us?

That called for another round.

Each of the four looked around the restaurant wondering if paranoia was contagious. An octogenarian two tables over with the wraparound sun glasses of the old was the only suspicious person any of them saw.

Liz broke the silence. "You know, I think Thanksgiving at the lake house would be perfect for the two of you. You've both been working very hard, no time off since the summer, what a great time for the two of you. Fire in the stove, walks in the woods and the beach. Lions on Thanksgiving." Liz couldn't help herself, Alex's hatred of football was well known. "Karen?"

"Perfect. It's Tuesday. Let's see if we can get you out next Monday or Tuesday, do it with fanfare like it's been planned forever and get you to Michigan because you want to celebrate Thanksgiving there."

Alexandra Kennedy and Wilson Bennett looked at each other. "Wish You Were Here" read the postcard.

"Cowboy, you're not going alone so if we're doing this, we're doing it together. End of story."

The four said their good-byes and Will and Alex walked back to the townhouse, got a glass of wine, got rid of their clothes, and retreated to the hot tub.

"Let's say the four of us are right and it really is Sam trying to get hold of us," Will started. "Why now? He's been gone over a year, neither hide nor hair with every cop in the country looking for him. And probably a bunch of crazy Russians. Why risk it?"

Alex. "Unless something's changed. Out of money? People closing in? Maybe thinking he's in the clear? But then why the postcard to Liz? Why not just call you?"

"Not a friggin' clue, Alexandra." Both lost in thought for some minutes, then out of the tub, into the shower and then into their favorite robes. Another glass of wine and early to bed.

CHAPTER THIRTY THREE
SAM

The rest of the week went quickly. Operating with the same healthy sense of paranoia, plans for the two to go to Michigan for Thanksgiving were made very public to the firm, the court and friends. There was nothing more from Michigan, no calls, no postcards, no nothing.

Alex and Will pondered what they would do once they got to the lake house. If Sam were there, how would he know they were? And was he still in danger? If yes, then would they be in danger as well? There was a .38 at the house, compliments of one of Kennedy's driving trips from Albuquerque to Michigan. Will didn't have a clue where she'd put it but both of them felt no small comfort knowing it was there if they needed it.

As the days dwindled to the Tuesday before Thanksgiving, the two were consumed by the questions that had no answers and grew increasingly impatient for the departure day to come. And when finally it did, they were at the airport two hours early for the earliest flight out, with boarding passes in hand and no luggage to check. Just ahead of the busiest travel weekend of the year, Will and Alex had the benefit of a seat between them but both needed to be touching the other for whatever was to come. An early season snow storm snarled Minneapolis air traffic and a 45 minute layover stretched to two hours before they finally took off for Michigan. Now ahead of the storm but at best by a day, they got a rental car at the airport and headed to the shore. Provisions at the last town for the next couple of days and then the last road, the last turn and the beauty of Lake Michigan, now grey and cold with clouds heavy in the air and daylight soon to be gone.

With all four arms filled with groceries and bags, Alex and Will staggered to the door, got it open, and went in. Alex went up the stairs, Will into the front room downstairs to turn the water pump and hot water heater on. Except that they already were on. Which was impossible.

Alexandra Kennedy screamed.

Will took the steps three at a time and came up beside his wife standing at the top. Across the living room seated in one of the leather recliners was the body of Sam Greenberg, clearly very dead, the back of his head gone, a 9mm Glock in his lap. There is this moment of facing something so incredibly horrific that the brain simply has to take long enough to grasp and assimilate what it is seeing. And so for those few seconds, both Alex and Will simply stood next to each other. Will noticed his friend's appearance, much thinner, a beard and hair dyed black, he was wearing an old flannel shirt and Michigan sweat pants that had been in Will's closet. Alex took in the blood and brain matter on the back of

167

the chair and on the carpet behind the chair and on the glass slider behind the chair, a vodka bottle on its side by the chair, Sam's eyes open to nothing ever more.

Finally, Alex whispered. "Will, we need to call 911." Will Bennett, finally coming to the realization that he had found his friend, fulfilled his quest, only to find him dead, came out of his dream. "Not yet."

He moved forward into the room. "Will, do not touch a thing!" Like his having lived there for 30 years wouldn't somehow reveal a few Bennett fingerprints. He nodded yes and circled the body. Clearly the gun had been in Greenberg's mouth when it went off and the bullet had gone through the back of his head leaving a gaping exit wound and the blood and brain tissue. He took in the vodka bottle and turned to the kitchen, noting everything was in its place. Walking past the kitchen to look into the bedroom, also spotless.

It took him a second to realize what was so very right about this scene and what had been so wrong at the Greenberg house a year ago. If Sam Greenberg had somehow gotten from Virginia to Michigan and had set up residence at the lake house, the one thing that wouldn't have changed was Sam's OCD. And it hadn't. Everything in its place, almost too perfectly, even for Sam.

"Will, come here." Alex quietly.

Will went back into the living area to find his wife standing over the dining table. In the midst of the table was a note written on a legal pad, a pencil beside it.

And in the same block printing as the post card. "RACHAL   I AM SO SORRY FOR EVERYTHING DADDY"

Will read the note again, took his bandana out of his back pocket to pick up the phone to call 911 and then looked again at the note.

Sam Greenberg had spelled his daughter's name wrong.

CHAPTER THIRTY FOUR
AFTERMATH

The four county patrol cars arrived very quickly especially given the remoteness of the lake house. Within 15 minutes, Alex and Will watched the progression of cars, lights flashing, come down the road, two into the driveway and two at the base of the hill. Two uniforms at the door for Will to let in, two more circling to the back, four more by their cruisers at the bottom. Guns were drawn initially and then put away as the officers secured the house and assured themselves that there were no bad guys lurking in the closets. Only a dead suicide in the living room.

Earnest and serious, the three men and one woman deputy were careful not to touch or disturb anything. It was clear to both Alex and Will that all four of them were trying to keep their respective composures in light of the dead stranger in the recliner. For Will Bennett, there was an odd calmness about him as the enormity of what had happened and what was going to happen sunk in. For Judge Kennedy, she had seen her share of crime scene and accident photos but nothing had prepared her for the smell of death. They would learn much later that Sam Greenberg had died within hours of their arrival and, even though the house was kept at a cool 45 degrees when they weren't there, the smell of death was everywhere from the faint trace of gunshot to the changes taking place in Greenberg's body.

Within the hour, more cars, marked and unmarked arrived. Detectives, Michigan State Police, medical examiner, crime scene people all setting up to do their jobs. Kleig lights were set up around the house. Will and Alex were kept in a separate bedroom downstairs apart from the "crime scene" and interviewed both separately and together. Finally, about 11 p.m., Michigan State Police Captain Blackman who was now in charge told them he had gotten them a room in town and that they were free to go. Exhausted beyond belief, they got to the rented car and silently left what had, until a few hours ago, always been the safest of havens. They found the motel in town, got the key from the office, opened the door to the Spartan simplicity of a bed, a bathroom with towels that were better suited to be bath mats, plastic cups for water, a two cup coffee maker, a TV with cable and little else.

Wordlessly, they dropped clothes worn now for a lifetime, took a hot shower, crawled into bed and held each other like never before. Arms and legs and toes and fingers and faces and lips and hairs and every possible way to physically touch. Not sexual, not this night, just surviving.

They began to talk and it lasted for hours. Alex was initially certain it was suicide, the theory of Sam finding out about the affair, killing his wife, running God knows how,

171

ending up at the lake house and, finally, overcome with the exhaustion and despair of always being on the run, sending the postcard and ending his life with the gun she was certain would be Sharon Greenberg's murder weapon.

Sam was initially just as certain that it was not suicide but homicide, on the wing and a prayer of knowing Sam for a lifetime and knowing he would never leave a whisker of his life out of place especially not killing himself with a gun that splattered brains all over the living room of a sanctuary as important to him as the lake house. His theory was that "others" (Russians, robbers, enemies) had killed Sharon Greenberg with Sam's gun, framed him, and he had spent the year running from whomever was after him. He knew the holes all too well. But he just couldn't believe that his best friend had killed his wife, run for a year, and then killed himself. Leaving a mess.

Sometime about four in the morning, Will got up to get a glass of water and pee and it all sank in. All the horror of the last hours, the last year, the phone call from Rachel about her mom. Sam so dead, his head gone, dressed in Will's clothes. He sat down on the toilet and began to cry … and cry and cry. Alex found him asleep on the floor on the bath map about an hour later. She got him back to bed and curled herself around him to keep him warm and safe until the morning arrived an hour later.

Will woke groggy about 7 to the ring of his cell phone.

"'Lo?"

"Will, it's Robert. Just got off the phone with the Staties. I'm sorry, man. I am so sorry. At National waiting on a flight that gets me in around noon. Got the last car anybody had to rent and I'll be there. Kids are with Rebecca for Thanksgiving and I needed a place to be. Might as well be Michigan. Catch me a room if you can."

Bennett welled. "Done, Robert. Thanks." And hung up.

Alex, awake now too, looked at him. And for the first time since he'd seen Sam, he smiled. "Cavalry's on the way."

They went back to bed for a little drifting and then up to face the day. They had a long breakfast at the Kountry Kitchen, local news talking about the suicide, feed ins to NBC and the suspicions that Sam Greenberg had killed his wife, the discovery of the body by Wilson Bennett, the owner of the home, the investigation ongoing, blah blah blah.

"Will?" Now lingering over coffee, eggs and American fries long gone.

"Alex, I just don't know. This is so beyond real. So beyond real." The last almost to himself. "More questions than before we got here."

"And seeing Sam dead?" Now there's the 800 pound gorilla.

173

He thought for a second almost guilty for what he was about to say.

"I'd already lost him somewhere between then and now." Pause for a breath. "So somehow seeing him yesterday was…anticlimactic? Ambivalent? Too weird for words? Something. And now somewhere between dead and numb. Like with Sy Silver at the hotel. What is wrong with me?"

She reached across the table. "Just walling off to hold off the pain and maybe later it will all come out and we'll deal with it then. But for now maybe peace?"

"Alex. Somebody killed him. I know it." Alex did an internal eye roll. Jesus.

A call on Will's cell from Captain Blackman asking for a meeting at the lake house at 2:00 P.M. saved Alex having to say anything. Will agreed and told the Captain that Detective Sergeant Davison from the Alexandria Police would also be there. Blackman, operating under the theory that another cop was a shit load better than lawyers, welcomed the news.

"See you there, Mr. Bennett."

"Yes sir."

CHAPTER THIRTY FIVE
THE CAVALRY

Davison called when he got to the airport and Bennett gave him directions to the motel. An hour later and a half hour before the meet with the Captain, there was a knock at the door. Alex opened it grateful beyond words for Robert's presence. They hugged at the door, Alex suddenly a bit breathless, and Davison, himself a half bubble off emotional balance, into the room to hug his friend. Bennett clueless.

They moved Davison into his room, told him what they knew, and got in the car to go to the lake house. On the way, he told them that he'd gotten a call from Captain Blackman around midnight telling him what they had found. Blackman had been careful in what he had said but impressed Davison both with his competence and his initial conclusion that this was a suicide of a wife killer. Case closed. And so Davison had gotten a flight first thing catching the last seat on a regional direct flight on the day before Thanksgiving. "Turns out Michigan in November isn't exactly a Mecca," said Davison.

When they arrived, both Will and Alex were stunned by the activity. Several marked patrol cars from the county, three from the Michigan State Police, two CSI vans, a canine unit, and enough police tape to build a house. They were ordered to park some distance away just as the first snowflakes began to fall. Escorted to the back door by a uniform, they were met at the door by Captain Blackman. He ushered them in and sat them downstairs in the family room introducing himself to Robert and a woman detective named Eileen Wolf to all three of them.

Blackman, looking tired and clearly wanting to get home, quickly got to the point.

"Judging by what's here, we think Greenberg had been here since roughly Labor Day. Makes sense, waiting for the tourists to leave, and having a little more safety. We've found a deer path with plenty of footprints over the dune and out to the county road leading to town. We've got people in town interviewing grocery stores. Unfortunately, all we have is a picture of the corpse and one that Alexandria police sent us this morning without the beard. Theory is that he lived here in total isolation, no lights to alert anybody, bought supplies in town and either hitch-hiked, biked or simply walked them in."

Wolf broke in. "We found several hundred dollars in cash in one of the drawers in the bedroom. Don't know where it came from but enough to get by for a while. Preliminary ballistics on the gun strongly suggests it's the gun that killed Sharon Greenberg."

Blackman again. "We looked at the report from a year ago and think he came here because it was the only place that he thought he could live in safety. No clue where he was up to a few weeks ago. And then as the weeks went by and he realized that there was no safety…ever…he liquored up and finished what he'd started." Not meaning to be mean but the words cut to Bennett's soul.

And then it suddenly dawned on him. Neither Alex nor Will had told the police about the postcard. Everybody thought that Kennedy and Bennett had come to Michigan for Thanksgiving and only Alex, Will, Karen and Liz knew differently. He felt his wife's eyes on him and knew that she knew.

Wolf went on about the investigation but Bennett and Kennedy were elsewhere trying to put the postcard some place in the mix. In sync as they so often found themselves, neither willing to offer it up just yet.

Wolf was winding up. "We have a lot to do, autopsy results, lots of prints and stuff here we have to process but the working theory is that Sam Greenberg killed his wife, somehow disappeared for almost a year, somehow got here, and finally decided that there was nothing else to do except end it." Almost as an afterthought. "We'll be done here hopefully by Sunday or Monday." So much for Thanksgiving dinner at the lake house, thought Will, although he truly wondered if he could ever come back and love this place as the sanctuary it had been.

177

Blackman stood, announcing the end of the meeting. He looked first at Davison and then at Alex and Will and then back to Davison. "We'll keep you posted." Which is to say we'll keep Davison posted and what he does with it is his business.

Now almost four in the afternoon, stuck in a couple of motel rooms in a town that after Labor Day closed for the year, the trio looked for a friendly bar in a deepening snow storm.

And found one.

Huddled into a booth, Bloody Mary's on order and a bowl of peanuts in front of them, Will Bennett looked at Alex, looked at Davison, and said.

"We've got something to tell you."

CHAPTER THIRTY SIX
FULL DISCLOSURE

"This is what we know. A week ago, we got a postcard." Alex pulled it out of her purse and gave it to Robert. He took it, read it, turned it over a couple of times, read it again, and laid it on the table, Alex thinking this is like Season's only colder. Davison looked at both of them, a cop now more than a friend.

"Why didn't you tell Blackman?"

Silence. The two feeling a little sheepish, a little like kids caught in a white lie and neither really understanding why it hadn't come up. Almost in unison, they both shrugged. "Don't know."

Will started. "A couple of more things. For a lifetime I've never known Sam Greenberg to leave anything out of order. And each time we're close to him, we find a scene so out of whack with who he was, that it simply makes no sense. He would never shoot himself in the head and leave others, probably me, to find it. Never.

One more thing." Will paused for a little dramatic effect.

"He spelled his daughter's name wrong."

Silence.

Davison asked, "Has anybody called her?"

Alex said that the officers had told her last night that they had gotten hold of her and told her. The deputy had remarked that there was no emotion, no affect in the young woman's voice when she had heard the news, only a 'Thank you for calling'.

Another round of Bloodys and they were no closer to answers than Will and Alex had been a week ago when it had all started. Exhausted now, all of them, they decided to quit talking about it and make plans for the weekend. A long nap was in order, then dinner at their favorite tavern, and thoughts about celebrating Thanksgiving if anything was going to be open.

Back to the "Motel Green Frog" as they had dubbed it for the very worn green exterior décor and promises to gather in a couple of hours.

Naked and under the covers and safe with Alex, Wilson Bennett finally allowed himself the finality of knowing his best friend of over 30 years was dead. In his head, he had come to grips with it for months but his heart had always left a window of hope. And now that was gone.

She held him close, skin to skin. His breathing slowed and deepened almost immediately, a talent that used to drive Alex crazy when he could fall asleep practically in the middle of an argument.

Alex awake, listening to his breathing, grateful to the goddess this time for his rest.

Somewhere between waking and drifting, an idea so preposterous she almost laughed out loud. An idea that she turned over in her head and then turned it again and again until she convinced herself that just maybe there were some legs to it. Awake now with sleep nowhere close, she lay next to her husband and began to work it through.

Two hours later, she got out of bed to go to the bathroom and noticed inches of snow now covered the parking lot of the Green Frog. Returning to the bedroom, Will was awake and paradoxically "ready". And so was she.

CHAPTER THIRTY SEVEN
ALEX

They knocked on Robert's door at eight, walked through what looked now to be about six inches of snow to the car and carefully made their way the roughly five or six miles to the inn, a horse livery in its prior 19th century life. Will drove as neither Alex of Albuquerque nor Robert of Alexandria had a clue how to drive in snow. They were rewarded by warm lights and early Christmas decorations and got a table by the fire. Drinks ordered and received, food order put off for awhile, Alex looked at the love of her life and at the man who somehow had also found a place in her heart.

"Gentlemen, I want to run something by you."

For half an hour, the two men remained silent as she ran through a scenario that was implausible and horrific and with almost no facts to support it. Even as she spoke, she recognized the flaws in her theory. But she pressed on and was delighted to see she had both of them captured by what she had to say. When she had finished, a second round of drinks had appeared as a gift from the owners, and they took a moment to order.

The three of them were silent then, each going over what Alex had proposed and each with their own thoughts. Alex, still recognizing it was a theory up to now made up by a mad woman who couldn't fall asleep next to her husband, but still thinking it had legs. Turning it over again and again.

Will Bennett on the one hand wanting to believe it because it was his best friend even though it painted a picture of a man that he had never known and, on the other, thinking it was pretty far out there. Robert Davison, the cop, drawn to this woman, this wife of his new friend, also thinking it was out there but already going back over the investigation that had lasted months and wondering if Alex's theory filled in some of the holes that they had never been able to fill and wondering how he could ever put a case together that would have any chance of getting a prosecutor to charge it.

It was finally Robert who broke the silence. "Let's say just for the sake of argument, you're right or mostly right. How would it ever get put together?" He went over the obvious points. "Sam Greenberg disappears for over a year with every law enforcement agency in the world looking for him and he winds up dead in what for all the world looks like a suicide with the same gun that he bought and that had killed his wife. That's number one. Number two, he runs off with all of the money from every joint account the couple had and we can't find a trace of it other than a few hundred dollars in cash at your house. Three, we think he was doing some heavy gambling with some very bad people which is a very good motive for raiding the family coffers."

183

Alex paused. "I don't think he took the money. I don't think to the day he died, he ever knew it was missing."

Dinner arrived and they ate quietly, each gathered and surrounded in their own thoughts. Every few minutes, one of them would raise a question and the three of them would ponder and discuss. Some could be answered. Some couldn't and some might never be. The two questions that were the hardest were these: If he hadn't taken the money and the Russians didn't have it, where was it? And the one that Will Bennett kept coming back to was why would he ever kill himself like that knowing who would find him? There was a third question that Will still struggled with and that was the disarray in the Greenbergs' bedroom. And what was he missing?

But as the night wore on and they retired to the bar area and had a night-cap or two, they began to think about what could be done to prove the unprovable.

Now at least ten inches of snow on the ground they made their way back to the motel still brainstorming, still questioning, still wanting to believe it was something other than what it looked like.

Will successfully negotiated the drive back to the motel, thankful, given the buzz he had, that the county mounties were either still at the lake house investigating the death of his best friend or saving motorists less skillful than he in the Thanksgiving Eve blizzard.

As they got out of the car heading to their respective rooms, Robert left them with this.

"It's the money trail." Hugs and to bed.

CHAPTER THIRTY EIGHT
PLOWING OLD GROUND

Alex Kennedy woke the next morning to a headache born of one too many Jameson's after dinner. When will I ever learn? And then rethought it. Everything in moderation including moderation, right? Knowing she'd probably do it again a time or two. She turned slightly and was startled to find Will Bennett staring at her.

"Been up long?" Sarcasm with a smile.

"Alex, why did he misspell Rachel's name? He knew we'd be the ones to find him. And why the mess in the bedroom in Virginia. What is he telling us?" Shook his head just enough to remind himself of the one too many Jameson's after dinner. Painful but curable. He'd had worse.

They had been two of the imponderables the night before. Only a few options. One, whoever had killed Sharon thought the place looked too neat and wanted to make it "more natural." Two, Sam had been at the house the morning his wife died and wanted to leave a clue that something was amiss but with no real reason to believe somebody who knew about the OCD would even be at the house. Three, the lake house misspelling was also a clue left for Will to find. Which made sense with the post card. But a clue to what?

Will got out of bed and checked through the curtain. The snow had stopped in the night and an early morning full moon lit up the motel landscape.

He turned back to Alex who was still working around her headache.

"Happy Thanksgiving." Sarcasm without the smile.

"Happy Thanksgiving, darling." She looked at her husband for a minute. "We'll get through this too, you know."

Will nodded absently and padded off to the bathroom to make some coffee.

They waited as patiently as they could but, after twenty minutes, Will went and knocked on Davison's door. He was already dressed with a cup of coffee in his hand, looked at the parking lot and announced that they'd be snowed in for days.

"You're not in Kansas anymore, Robert," Will said. "I'm guessing roads are clear and flights are flying. Get your coat and let's find breakfast."

The best they could do was a McDonald's on Thanksgiving morning and the threesome allowed themselves the luxury of eating in. Greenberg's death, the violation of the sanctity of the lake house, and the excitement of testing Alex's theory led to a unanimous decision, - get it cleared with Blackman and find their way back to Virginia the sooner the better. Davison accomplished the first, cop to cop, and left it that Blackman would call him with the results of the investigation of the house and the autopsy and anything else of import. Alex got hold of the airline with the startling news to her and Robert that indeed the flights were flying and that there was a regional jet into National leaving in three hours with plenty of seats available on the one day when nobody ever needs to fly.

In a rush, they got back to the Motel Green Frog, got packed and caravanned back to the airport. Davison following, initially a little intimidated by the amount of white stuff on either side of the road but settling in with little problem once they got to the expressway.

Seven hours to the minute from breakfast at McDonalds on the shores of Lake Michigan, Alex and Will were checked into the Holiday Inn "back home again" in the middle of Alexandria. Robert dropped them off for a night alone and with a promise to reconvene in the morning at the police department to plow old ground.

Alex and Will were left to their own devices and settled for the Holiday Inn Restaurant thankfully just before the "live" music and with enough of a Thanksgiving buffet and a couple of Jameson's and some wine to calm the seas.

Most of the trip east, Will had been chewing on the last year and wondering where the pieces fit, still nagged by what he was missing. He had started with the Alexandria house the morning of the visit with the cops and Rachel and replayed the scene again and again. There was something not quite right with it, not big, not just quite right. Fast forward through the initial investigation with Davison and Olstrom, he remembered seeing an inventory of the master bedroom and bathroom, all seemingly in order…except … something. The months that went by, returning to a normalcy that wasn't quite right. The horror at the lake house, Bennett knowing he had to do something with Sam's remains because there was nobody else in the world who would and remembering to call Blackman the next Monday to figure out what to do once the M.E. was done with the autopsy. Replaying the scene in the living room with Sam's body going frame by frame over what had been his true brother.

And then, sometime between the first and second Irish, and the salad bar and the stuffing, now cold and congealed on the buffet, he thought he remembered. His first thought was how stupid he was to have taken this long to remember and his second, whether it made any difference at all.

Alex, alone and quiet in her own thoughts at the table, startled by her husband. "Alex, play this out with me."

CHAPTER THIRTY NINE
GLORY DAYS

"A thousand years ago when we were in Florida, somebody, wife, lover, doesn't matter, took a picture of the two of us. We'd just played some tennis and had kicked the shit out of some cocky teenagers from Ohio. It was one of those great pics when life is good and everything is in front of you so we had a couple of 8 X 10s made, you know, the one on my bookcase at the office. And a couple of smaller ones that each of us put in plastic and kept in our Dopp kits. The idea was that it was always a reminder of what we meant to each other. And it was always a part of us. Do you remember it? And Sam had his on his desk as well. We both kept the little ones with us when we traveled."

"So?"

"That morning at the house with Rachel, Davison and Olstrom? It wasn't there."

"Where?"

"In his Dopp kit. He had it pinned to the top, in the little plastic frame just like the one I have. Always. But that morning it was gone."

"How can you know that for sure, Will? Major league stress, best friend gone, best friend's wife dead, total freak out scene. And you think you noticed a little picture of the two of you was gone. Seriously?"

Will gave up on the stuffing and settled for his Jameson's. "Yep. Worse yet, darling, I'm betting that when I call Blackman tomorrow morning, he'll tell me he found the picture either on Sam's body or somewhere at the lake house."

Alex, the "Return of the Headache" from the morning beginning to lurk in the not so deep recesses of her mind, asked the obvious.

"So what? Doesn't that just mean he was there that morning, killed his wife, took the picture because it reminded him of the two of you before things got so screwy, and then split? Aren't you just digging his grave deeper?" It was one of those thoughts that ought to stay in the bubble over your head or one of those phrases you'd like to have back before anybody hears it. But then she looked at Will who was already near choking with laughter. And then her too. After all, how much deeper can it get? He's dead. And totally embarrassing themselves by needing to leave the crowded dining room to go outside together to get some air practically holding each other up with tears streaming down their faces. Blessed relief from tension too thick to cut. They finally getting back to the dining room, now drawing dubious glances from other diners or travelers who thought the Thanksgiving Buffet at the Alexandria Holiday Inn was where it's at and clearly disturbed by the two recently escaped mental patients.

Quieter finally. "So what?" Where it all started.

191

"This. He was there that morning or at least close on to Sharon's murder. He takes the only thing he cares enough about to take without raising suspicion. The picture."

"Jesus, Will. He kills his wife and wants to disappear forever getting away from the cops who he knows thinks he killed his wife, getting away from the Russians who will kill him on sight, getting away with God knows how much cash he's taken from the accounts. So he takes the one thing that reminds him of better times. So fucking what?"

"I don't think that's what happened. I think he's there that morning, finds his wife dead, either knows for sure or thinks he knows what happened but knows for sure that he is so on the hook for it that he knows he has to run, disturbs the scene by making it look like my room might look, takes the picture and makes a run for it."

"Back to the Russians?"

"Au contraire. Back to me."

"Call Blackman tomorrow on the picture thing, will you?"

"First thing."

They finished "dinner" and wandered back to the room, both quiet with their own thoughts. Alex thinking Will was a tad farther out there on the picture thing and Will thinking that he had figured out one more piece of the puzzle.

To bed in the spoon that they so loved and soon both into a very deep sleep, part exhaustion, part Jameson's.

CHAPTER FORTY
FOLLOW THE MONEY I

7:00 a.m. came early and both awoke to the sound of the room phone. Robert Davison on the other end announcing that, rather than meeting at the police station, he would stop by his office, box up the file, and come to the motel.

"Why the change in plans, Robert?" Alex asked.

"I want to follow the money trail and I don't want Olstrom to know what I'm up to. He's the one who ran that piece of the case and, if he's there, he'll know we're looking at what he did."

Fair enough. Will and Alex showered and dressed and helped themselves to the sumptuous breakfast "express." Juice, bagels, doughnuts, and a banana that had seen better days. The Friday after Thanksgiving and not even turkey leftovers. Davison found them in the lounge, helped himself to the feast, loaded up with coffee, went back to his car to get the three banker's boxes representing the Greenberg file and then showed up at the room.

The three of them spent most of the morning concentrating on the financial records from the various banks and the brokerage house that represented the savings and retirement plans for the Greenbergs. Olstrom had gotten search warrants for the various accounts and all confirmed what they had known for over a year. All but the checking account had been cleaned out. Just north of 2.5 million dollars. Will was not particularly surprised. Sam had done well over the years and had gotten a modest inheritance from his mother and father. It was certainly enough to get Rachel through school and enough left over for retirement some years down the way.

To Davison's everlasting chagrin, it was Alex Kennedy who first realized what was missing. She thought about it for a minute and looked both at Davison and Bennett.

Bennett met her eyes. "What?"

"Robert, did you bring the statement file?"

"Sure, it's right here." He went to one of the boxes on the bed and pulled out the file that contained the various statements they had taken from Rachel, from family friends, from Will Bennett, from co-workers.

And then Davison got it. Both Alex and Robert now looking at Will.

"What? What?"

Davison took a breath. "He never talked to anybody. At the banks, at the brokerage house, at the insurance company. He fucking never talked to any of them." Clearly very very angry. And not just a little embarrassed too.

Bennett, surprised first at Davison's use of profanity, slowly got to where Alex and Robert already were.

"They were all joint accounts, weren't they?"

195

Davison nodded.

The three of them sat silently for what seemed like several minutes. It was finally Will who broke the silence.

"What if Sam didn't take the money?"

Davison. "Then Alex is right, Will."

They took a break then, realizing they were now closing in on something very big. Davison was on his cell calling the banks and Merrill Lynch, Will calling back to Michigan on his cell to talk to Captain Blackman, Alex pondering the two of them silently lost in her own thoughts.

Bennett done first. "They have the oral report from the M.E. Gunshot wound to the head. Massive damage to the brain, death instantaneous." He paused.

"Wallet?"

"Nothing much. No driver's license, no credit cards. Some local business cards at the lake that he must have shopped in." He paused for what he hoped was a dramatic moment. "He was holding the picture of the two of us in his hand."

Kennedy nodded and smiled. Another piece. She wasn't sure what it meant or where it went but another piece nevertheless.

Davison hung up. "Friday after Thanksgiving not exactly the perfect time to get hold of people but the Greenberg's broker is in today. I'm on my way. Join me?"

Kennedy and Bennett went for their coats.

They arrived at the broker's office in Arlington just after 1:00 p.m. Cynthia Hollingsworth was waiting for them. In her early 50s, she was the quintessential stock broker. Professional, well dressed, to the point. By way of history, she had known the Greenbergs for twenty years and had been responsible for the Greenberg portfolio up until roughly late August, three months before Sharon Greenberg's death.

Davison taking the lead. "What happened?"

Hollingsworth had at first been reluctant to talk to the detective in the presence of Kennedy and Bennett but it didn't take much persuading once she understood why they were there and once she understood she was a search warrant away from having to do it anyway.

"Late August a year ago, Sharon came in and said that she and Sam had talked about it and were deciding to move their portfolio elsewhere. Apparently, they had a relative who was starting out and they wanted to help her."

"Twenty years and all of a sudden, they pull the plug?'

Circumspect, Hollingsworth said, "It happens."

"Transfer? Or sell it all and start over?"

"That was the weird part. Sell it all to start all over again."

"Did that make any sense at all to you?"

"Fifteen months ago was the downturn. In the long run, it was stupid to sell off but in the short run, there were at least major losses that would help their taxes."

"Give her any advice at all?"

Hollingsworth, quietly. "No."

"How did she seem?" Davison asked.

"Fine. Just like always. Very apologetic, very gracious in terms of how much I'd done for them. But they just thought for the sake of family unity, they should do this. I gave her a form for Sam to fill out and she was back the next day with it all signed."

"Did you verify his signature?"

"I did. Compared it to the signatures we had on file for him. No question it was his."

"Call him?"

She paused for more than a second. "It never dawned on me. I'd known them forever. They were friends. Had been for a long time. We socialized, went to parties, they helped me through my divorce." Another pause. "What's this about? He killed her, right? For the money?" And then it began to sink in. She looked again at her file, looked at the signatures, and suddenly understood why these three strangers were sitting across from her.

Proper, professional, money manager for the rich.

"Oh, Christ."

"Exactly. How much?"

"I authorized a certified check to the two of them for 1.6 million after I sold it all off. Took a couple of days."

"Losses?"

Hollingsworth looked at her computer screen, pushed a few buttons, and then said, "Right around $275,000." Even quieter.

Kennedy couldn't restrain herself. "A relationship that you had had with the two of them for twenty years, one of the two walks into your office one day and announces they're liquidating two million dollars taking a $275,000 hit, you get a proxy from the husband, and you're OK with that?" Ironic incredulity a trademark both off and on the bench. "Didn't you even have to clear it with somebody? Jesus."

To her credit, Hollingsworth stayed composed. She looked at all three of them, stood up and walked out of the room.

"Nice touch, Judge." Her husband.

Kennedy had finally had enough. Over a year of pain, uncertainty and having half a husband. Walking in on a dead man at the lake house, strange feelings about a cop half a country away, now a theory that was growing more legs every minute. Bennett should have known better.

Scarily calm now. Will knew this part of her. Robert was about to find out.

"Two nights ago, we drank too much and talked about a scenario that was totally off the wall. Ever since then, everything we've touched is one more piece. We will talk to the banks and they will tell us that Sharon Greenberg, on joint accounts, with Sam Greenberg's signature, closed the accounts and took certified checks made payable to the two of them. We will call the insurance agency and they will tell us Sharon Greenberg, with Sam Greenberg's written authorization, cashed in her own policy. Thirteen days before she died. And do you know what else that insurance agency will tell us? Sam Greenberg's life insurance was paid up full.

"Sharon Greenberg wasn't supposed to die that day. It was supposed to be Sam." Almost a whisper. Each word a sentence.

"Gentlemen, there are two endings to this story, neither of which we likely will ever prove. Certainly not beyond a reasonable doubt. But it will be enough for us."

"Alex? We've got to talk to Captain Young. I know what you're thinking. And I'm with you. But we can't do a rogue cop rogue judge thing. Even if you are from New Mexico." Davison stopped long enough to at least get a smile out of her. And he did.

Friday night at the police station, they met with Alicia Young for three hours and laid it all out. She wanted proof and they had none. She wanted a bullet proof plan and they

201

didn't have one. She wanted judicial cover and there was no way any judge would give them what they needed. She wanted state police help and that was a political impossibility.

So it was Chief Alicia Young, Detective Sergeant Davison, a cowgirl judge from New Mexico, and a lawyer who would do anything to save what was left of the legacy of his friendship with Sam Greenberg.

Young looked at Davison, a cop bond ever too strong. She looked at Kennedy and especially Bennett and understood more than anybody the need for closure.

"You're covered. Get it done."

She stood up, wrote down the name of a cop they would need where they were going, gave it to Davison, and told them she would call and tell him they were coming. And left.

The three of them sat down to figure it all out. It depended on Monday and the bank and the life insurance company, the end of the Thanksgiving weekend, and time to make a plan.

Too jazzed to go to bed, they went to the local watering hole where Robert and Will had gone the night of Silver's death and found a booth. Mostly empty, most of the regulars at home with their families, Reba on the box, they ordered drinks and grilled cheese and burgers and veggie burgers and fries. Then one more round.

The captain showed up. "Thought I'd find you here. Mind if I join you?" Of courses all around. "What you're thinking about doing is about to fuck this lovely little career up. Might as well be part of the solution." A very beautiful smile, a very class act.

They drank until it closed and then went to Sophie's for breakfast, coffee and some major sobering up. Bennett taking notes on anything he could find to write on which would be cocktail napkins he numbered, sure if he didn't, these great plans would be lost to the universe by morning's light. He'd had way too much experience solving the world's problems in way too many forums like this with way no recollection the next day to let it happen again. Captain Young the voice of reason for awhile and then clearly knowing this was the only chance they had.

About 4:00 a.m. Saturday, it was a plan that at least had a beginning and an end. They would rest on Sunday, fiddle with the details, and Monday try to make sense of it all. Then make a run at it.

Good-byes and hugs, Will barely remembering the last hours but firmly holding the cocktail napkins; Kennedy stone cold sober, scared to death about the next 48 hours, hoping the dawn would bring a change. Davison, red portable flashing on his unmarked marked assured to make it home after he dropped them off. And Young, after everything she'd been

203

through to be a black woman in a white man's world, now rolling the dice of her career for no other reason than it was a run at justice. And in the darkness before the dawn and with the home fries only half helping the buzz from the bar, she knew in her heart she was right to choose to do what had to be done.

Only later would she realize how wrong she could be.

CHAPTER FORTY TWO
A LAST DAY OF BEAUTY

Will and Alex woke the next morning around 10 again nursing Tylenol headaches, Will opening the blinds to bright and warm sunshine that staggered him backwards right back into bed. With not much urging, cautious and careful lovemaking followed that did more than the Tylenol to rid the pain and prepare them for the day.

Robert was busy with his kids and the two decided to take the day off and explore and re-explore the nation's Capital. In one of those strange interludes of quiet in busy lives when there is simply nothing to do but live, they promised themselves a day. Over "brunch", they talked about the days to come but mostly just enjoyed the moment. One of Will's great quotes was the John Lennon line: "Life is what happens while you're busy making other plans." They talked about how there is always one more thing in the way, one more trial to try, one more payment to make, one more something. Something. Something. This day they would try to do differently.

And so on a spectacularly beautiful Sunday, warm for late November in DC and with not a cloud in the sky, they walked the beauty of the city, did the Smithsonian, the Native American Museum, the National Art Gallery, and ended again with the haunting Memorials to all those who had given lives for the lives Alex and Will lived.

Back to Alexandria, Robert's favorite bar for dinner and early to bed.

Nobody ever knows how many sunsets they get. But if this was the last one, they had done it pretty good. Spooned. For what was to come.

CHAPTER FORTY THREE
MONDAY

Bright and early, Kennedy and Bennett were back on Mill Street with Davison planning out the day. Olstrom was back on the scene, obviously curious, either too stupid or too proud to ask, and kept a watchful distance. Robert, Will and Alex were in the conference room poring over documents, Robert taking a certain amount of pleasure in leaving the blinds open only to either appease or feed his anger by letting Olstrom know something was afoot.

The trio spent the morning making the rounds and confirming what they already knew. From banks to insurance agency and between, they confirmed that the only human contact, the only request, the only anything had come from Sharon Greenberg on behalf of both Sam and Sharon. All joint accounts, they had required Sam's signature but, because of the long standing nature of the various relationships, no thought was given by anyone to independently verify that indeed these were joint decisions. By mid afternoon, they confirmed that, over the period of several months before her death, Sharon Greenberg had wiped out every account they had, save for the day to day checking.

On the day of her death, Sharon Greenberg had in hand a lot of money. To this day nobody knew where it was.

They met back at police headquarters and counseled with Captain Young going over what they had learned, filling in more pieces of the puzzle, until they had down what, in their minds, had happened. Only they still didn't have any way to prove it.

Sandwiches and soft drinks in the conference room for dinner, Olstrom now looking half crazed on the outside looking in, the foursome planned it all out. At the end of the day, Bennett and Davison were "ayes"; Kennedy was a "nay"; Young abstained. Two to one, Kennedy with a very strong dissent.

It was time to put the plan in play.

Will went into a vacant office, fished out his cell phone, found the number in his crackberry, rehearsed a couple of times, and dialed.

Voice mail. The carefully rehearsed conversation, now message, was left with his request for a call back and his number. He hung up, heart beating a little too quickly, breath a little too fast, and went back to the conference room to report.

Beginning to wrap up, Will's cell phone rang and the four froze.

A very deep breath. He pushed the green light on his phone.

"Hey."

CHAPTER FORTY FOUR
THE UNION

After a long talk that taxed Will Bennett's persuasive skills to the max, they finally agreed to meet the next afternoon at 1 p.m. at the student union. He hung up with a feeling of terrible, sad, bone numbing fatigue and looked at the others.

"We're in play."

With Will and Alex mainly bystanders, the next several hours went by quickly. Young and Davison on their cell phones to avoid immediate tracings to the police station numbers, chits called in, pleas made, cajoling, begging, plans and back-up plans made. By 10, they were finished.

It would be what it would be.

Too wired to have a drink, too much on everybody's mind, they split up, Robert dropping Alex and Will off at the hotel, Young home. To meet the next morning to bring it home.

That night, Wilson Bennett slept as well as he had since that awful phone call just over a year ago. Alex Kennedy slept not a wink. For the longest time, she lay next to him, mulling over their history, their lives, scared shitless over what the next day would bring, wondering about the future if there were one to have, wondering about Davison and feelings for him, pissed off at the two of them for this ridiculous scheme they had concocted with no real end game in sight, realizing it was her idea that got it all started, pretty much generally just pissed off.

And then pissed off at Bennett going to sleep like he did all the time. And in what seemed like a very few seconds, she drifted, spooned, and the wakeup call.

Bennett, as always, oblivious to his wife's sleeping habits, woke energized, anxious for the day, and wanting desperately to make love. Alex was, after a very long night, hardly inclined. She said so and Will sulked and went to the shower.

In the days to come, it was a decision she regretted with every fiber of her being.

They dressed in silence, did a coffee and a bagel at the "express" and met Davison at the entrance in the marked unmarked. To the station for final plans to be made, phone calls to friends in the south to cash in the chits, Kevlar vest fitted, wires mounted, all systems checked, the rental car also wired, and the caravan ready to proceed, Will in the rental, Davison, Young and Kennedy in the trailer, two volunteer junior detectives in a third car, down I66 to Route 29 South.

When he got close, he drove around a bit to give Davison's people time to get placed. Bennett got to the union early but not by too much, found a table that was both public enough for his entourage and private enough to have the talk of his lifetime.

She arrived at exactly 1:00. Will rose to greet her, stunned by the changes he saw in her from first a grieving, devastated, lost young woman to the hatefulness she had shown towards him about her dad, to a very sophisticated, very well groomed, very together young woman.

He rose. "Rachel." No handshake, no hug. Just "Rachel". And in response, "Will".

They sat down, Will asked about something to eat, or coffee, and Rachel said no to both. It was very clear to Will that they were here to discuss what had to be discussed, end of discussion.

And so he started.

"There are blanks to be had, a bunch of which I'll never know. But I do know this. Last November, you killed your mom and last week you killed your dad."

A pause for dramatic effect, she blinked once, and otherwise nothing.

In for an ounce, in for a pound, Will began to gather steam.

"Your mom was having an affair and you found out about it, maybe encouraged it, maybe helped plot it, maybe just stood by and watched it happen. You found out maybe because she told you or maybe because you're smart.

You get pregnant, maybe the love of your life, maybe not." A flicker in her eyes and then back to the mask. "Mom insists on an abortion, you get it, and hate her for life. But mom doesn't know it, she thinks you are all doing the right thing.

And then maybe because she tells you and maybe because you're smart, you figure out she's robbing the family jewels to run away to be happy. Which might be OK except she's also running away from you. And the inheritance. That last summer the two of you confide like no other time in your life. Abortion forgotten, all past ills forgotten. She tells you what she's doing and about the money and where it is. Maybe she tells you she's going to kill your dad. Maybe not. But whatever, for her, past sins forgotten. Only they aren't. Because they can't be."

Bennett pauses, one to catch a breath, and two, to see how he's doing. Stone faced, impassive. No way to go but to get'er done.

"The money's in cash and you know where it is. Time is short and mom tells you about leaving. You go to school but know something has to be done. That night before or morning of, doesn't matter, you drive up from Charlottesville, park the car blocks away in the dark, wait for your dad to walk the dog like he always does, same time every morning, go in, know where your dad keeps the gun, walk into your mom's room, she's surprised, shocked, and you shoot her stone cold dead. Out the door, a few blocks to the car, back to Charlottesville and in time for class at 9. And by the way, you get the cash where she's stashed it.

Dad comes home, finds mom dead, can't find his gun, thinks it's the lover or a robber, but sure he'll get tagged and decides to run for it. But what you don't know because you're long gone is that he leaves clues that only a very few would listen to. Like leaving his underwear on the chair. What must you have thought when you walked in the room that day with the detectives and me and Alex and saw what he had done? And knew that I saw it too. You never knew about the picture of us that he had carried for thirty some years. So he left a mess and took the picture and hoped somehow that I'd get there and I'd notice. He did that and went on the run. I'm guessing with money he'd stashed for a rainy day.

Never for a second thinking you would've killed your own mom, he lived the next year God knows where and how. Hiding in dark corners, always hungry, always running. Every minute wondering how you were, but scared to get hold of you."

A little flush around the neck, still impassive, still saying nothing, and, now more than ever, Will knew Alex had been right.

"Some time not too long ago, he calls you, now living at the end of the line, and asks to meet with you at the only safe place he can think of. The lake house. You agree because he is a major loose end.

But he sends me a post card. Because he wants his best friend finally to know what's up.

The two of you meet, maybe you drove, maybe you flew, maybe you paid cash, maybe your professors noticed you weren't there right before Thanksgiving, but I'm pretty sure the cops can figure out a trip to Michigan for you just before the holiday. And your dad's dead. Same gun as killed your mom because you had it with you all the time. Maybe you're smart enough to convince him to kill himself or maybe you did it yourself. Doesn't matter really. You killed them both whether you pulled the trigger or not.

There were never any Russians, never any gambling, never your dad having affairs. Nothing. All made up by a very smart psychopath daughter. Was it your mom forcing you to have an abortion? Your dad being mean to you? Or just plain fucking greed so bad you'd kill your parents for it?"

Bennett now really running out of steam but needing to finish. This would be the sit down moment.

"So I'll go back to those hick cops in Alexandria, Davison, was that his name? Tell them what I have, and maybe they'll check your credit cards, or ask for bank statements, or whatever hick cops do. Maybe you made a mistake. Maybe your parents will have the justice they deserve."

They looked at each other for what seemed to Will to be forever. Rachel unblinking and so cold. She stood and so did he.

"You done?"

"For now."

And turned.

Beyond exhaustion, heartsick and weary to his very core. It had been the most important closing argument of his life.

And pure and simply, he had failed. Miserably and totally.

It was maybe a step or two, he would never know.

In those last split seconds, he heard two words, maybe three. The first, clearly Davison. "Police!! Drop it." And then maybe Alex, "Will!" Two pops, one like somebody kicked him in the kidney, the other to the back of his head, propelling it forward so his chin hit his chest. More pops.

Darkness, so deep as to be purple. So very deep.

He had lost.

215

CHAPTER FORTY FIVE
HARD TIMES

It had been six days since the shootings. Rachel Greenberg dead in a storm of police bullets a split second too late. Will Bennett clinging to life in the ICU of the UVA Health Systems, on a vent and medically induced coma, while the neurosurgeons waited for the swelling to calm before they could see what was left.

It had all gone to plan but for two things. One, Rachel Greenberg showed no expression at all while she was being accused of murdering her parents. Although, as Davison and Young put it together later, they should have known better. And two, she had a gun, a .22 caliber hand bag pistol, and wasn't afraid to use it to kill Will Bennett in a public place. The first shot hit him in the back, lodged in the Kevlar, and was of no consequence. The second hit him back in the head and, according to the surgeons, hit just above the brain stem. Which was why he was still alive. Sort of.

Once the name calling and political bullshit wrangling and turf struggles were out of the way, the Virginia State Police took over the investigation and put the rest of the pieces together. Rachel Greenberg had taken $2.3 million dollars and opened random accounts all over the Charlottesville area. Brokerage houses, banks, an on campus credit union. She had paid for her tuition, after the scholarships and grants, for the next three years of undergrad in cash, an event so unusual at the University of Virginia that they simply took the money and never asked a question. She lived a quiet but very comfortable life in a two bedroom off campus luxury apartment. No friends to speak of, no involvement with the University, all A's. She was clearly biding her time. The gun was traced to a downtown DC pawn shop, the reason for purchase was "Personal Protection", the background check pure, and she had paid in cash.

All of it would have worked save for a very smart New Mexico cowgirl judge and the bonds of a friendship forged in law school by two very different men and steeled by the journeys of life. Now one of those friends was cleared of his wife's murder but very dead and the other clinging to life. The ICU nurses would tell Alex that others far less injured would almost certainly have died but for Wilson Bennett, there was a will to live that surprised and challenged them and turned them into cheerleaders for a man they never really knew. They were concerned about the time on the vent, concerned about respiratory distress that could kill a patient all by itself. But for six days they did what ICU nurses did best. They cared.

On the morning of the seventh day, Robert Davison and Alex Kennedy got in the unmarked marked for the trip to the hospital. For the first five days they had stayed in separate rooms at the Holiday Inn Express, Judge Kennedy choosing not to stay in the hospitality hospital lodging. For the last two nights they had shared the suite, Robert in the living room on the couch and Alex in the bedroom. Nothing sexual, just the need to be closer, each deep in their own thoughts of all that had happened over the last six days, the last months, the last years. Kennedy thinking of a life without Will; Davison mulling life without his family and struggling with the guilt of a plan gone wrong.

They drove in silence to the hospital as they almost always did, parked in the visitor's lot and walked into the inevitability of another day of machines and sadness.

And when they got off the elevator, nothing much seemed different.

Until Audrey Simmons, charge nurse for the unit, and a woman Davison and Kennedy both had come to love and respect, approached, professional as always but this morning with tears in her eyes. She spoke to Alex, holding out her hand.

"Come with me, Judge."

CHAPTER FORTY SIX
ANYONE WHO DOESN'T BELIEVE IN
MIRACLES DOESN'T BELIEVE IN REALITY

Alexandra Kennedy had been through enough tragedy in her lifetime to know what the next moments would feel like. This would be worse, of course, because it was the man who was truly her soul mate. Yes, this would be the worst. And she got ready.

Except this time was different. Will Bennett was propped on pillows, eyes open, vent off, head bandaged, eyes black and blue and drowsy, IVs in both arms. But he turned his head when he saw her, eyes crinkled with tears.

"Hey cowgirl," his voice weak and hoarse but it was the most beautiful sound in the world to his woman. Audrey, two other nurses, the attending neurosurgeon, and two residents around the bed, voyeurs of the most private of moments but one they couldn't stand to miss.

Audrey told the story. After Davison and Kennedy had left the night before, the order had come to begin to lighten the medical coma. The medical staff had thought at least 24 and probably 48 hours before there would be, if at all, any improvement. But around 5:00 a.m. that morning, Will had begun to awaken. Audrey had been called and had come in early, not to manage, but to witness for herself one more miracle of life over death. Throughout the early morning, he had continued to strengthen, they had stopped the vent for the first time, and he took his first unassisted breaths, they had put him back on the vent for a time, and then began to wean him a few minutes each time.

When Audrey knew Alex was coming, she assembled the team that had come to care so dearly for Will Bennett, plumped and propped his pillows, cleaned him up a bit, told him what was happening, and made certain he was off the vent when they brought her in.

Alex took his hand in hers, self control for six days dissolved now in a joy like no other. "Hey Will. Welcome back."

Will nodded, tears freely flowing down his cheeks. A moment nurses and doctors and families live for.

Natasha Atkinson, the attending neurosurgeon, the woman who had saved her husband's life, called in especially for this, was the one to caution.

"There is more to be done, time to be back on the ventilator, more that could go wrong, more roads to travel." A pause. "But, as days go, this is a pretty damn good one."

Alex hugged her, now sobbing uncontrollably. The two held each other for a very long time, the one married to her man, the other the woman who had given him back to her.

From his bed, still quiet and still hoarse. "Robert?"

"I'll get him, Will."

Alex went out to the waiting room to get Robert heavily into a Peoples' from months ago. She said nothing, simply motioned him to follow.

Will Bennett watched him come into the room, had practiced the line at least twice, took a deep full breath that was his own.

"Can't you fuckin' do anything right, Detective?"

Davison, tears himself, without missing a beat. "Why the fuck didn't you just duck?"

Anyone who doesn't believe in miracles.

EPILOGUE
LAKE HOUSE
MEMORIAL DAY

Alone on the beach, the warmth from the day and the fading sun now far to the north of where it had been just six months ago when life had changed forever. Memorial Days in Michigan were weird, either the worst of snowstorms or the heat and sun of the season to come. This time they had gotten lucky.

He sat on the driftwood log on the beach and watched his best friend's ashes dissolve and disappear in the gentle swell of the lake they had both loved so much.

Quiet and peaceful, Will thought about the last months. They had not been easy. The bullet to his head had missed killing him by millimeters but was close enough for Dr. Atkinson to get to it and get it out. More concern about the swelling in the brain and the sudden thrust forward on his neck. As Bennett began to gather strength, it was his neck that had caused him the most trouble. It would be a constant struggle for a long time but a small price to pay and maybe even a little better today than yesterday. Miraculously, cognitive deficits had vanished once the swelling had gone down. Atkinson said it was the EMTs at the Union that had made all the difference.

Sitting there in the warmth of the fading sun, Will began to cry, remembering that last day when they had wheeled him out to the unmarked marked with Davison behind the wheel and his beloved Alex holding the door. He had asked the EMTs who had been at the union, Dr. Atkinson, and his nurses, especially the nurses, to be there. They had had a small reception with juice, coffee and cake and Will had tried to talk about what they all had meant to him. But he didn't get very far before Alex had to step in to finish. They watched him helped into the front seat for the trip to DC and then for the flight back to Albuquerque He had seen them wave good bye and then turn back to the hospital to do what they did best knowing that they had saved a life.

Davison and Young were given thirty day paid suspensions for breaking more rules than they knew existed. They were hailed as heroes both by their brothers and sisters on the force and by the local media. Olstrom was doing well on traffic duty and hoped one day to return to be a full fledged patrolman. The last time Will and Robert talked, Robert had talked about some social times with his captain ("Those would be called dates, Robert."). They were now both back on duty keeping Alexandria safe and northern Virginia was far better for it.

Will's mind turned to Rachel. The police had found a stack of journals when they searched her apartment going back to early high school. There had been a darkness about her that had gone undetected. Visions of death and destruction, hatred of herself and her parents. It was all very graphic and very violent. The one bright spot was an older man she had met someplace and who had gotten her pregnant. There were passages about a life together with their child, then devastation when he disappeared, then rage when her mother insisted on an abortion or she would be disinherited. So she had gotten the abortion and plotted her mother's death every day of her life until that cold November morning when it all came together. It was all so very awful and so very sad.

The money Rachel had stashed was recovered from the various accounts. She had left no will and there were no living relatives. With Will's input, the bulk of the money was given to the Anti Defamation League, Sam's passion for a lifetime, and enough left over for two other projects. One was an endowment to the Temple for a memorial in the name of Sam and Sharon Greenberg to further educational pursuits for young people. The second, an endowment for husbands and wives to get "healthy" counseling not to figure out what was wrong but what was right and how to keep it so. It had been Alex's idea. Healthy marriage counseling. What a concept.

Will thought about his friend and all that he had learned about him over the past months.

In many ways not the man Will Bennett thought he knew so well. But it really didn't matter. What mattered was that in the heartbeat of life, two men had found a friendship many go a life time without. That was good enough for Will. He would live with the memory of the Sam Greenberg he knew.

Will stood up, arranged the neck brace, and turned to the lake house. Grace was there with a new boyfriend from law school who even her dad liked.

And Alexandra Kennedy. She was there.

Wilson Bennett looked forward to the night ahead and to the next morning before the "kids" were up. Neck pain and all. And to all the days to come.

Ashes to the lake, memories forever, Will climbed the dune home.

Justice, Sam. We got you justice. And peace.

***

'And you can call on me until the day you die.'

About the Author

This is the first novel for Bill who has been a trial lawyer in West Michigan for over 35 years. "I've been living in a fantasy world most of my life. I thought I'd write some of it down."

Bill, his spouse Rebecca, and daughter Kate, two cats, two rabbits, and hopefully soon a dog, split their time between the Frog's Reach Farm in Montague, Michigan, and Grand Rapids.